THE PERFECT DISTRACTION

BOSSY HEARTS

BOOK 3

EVEY LYON

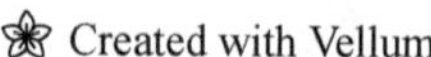 Created with Vellum

ABOUT

This boss is on a mission to distract her...

Wes Bay didn't mean to trick his little sister's best friend into working for him. Okay, he totally did, but he needs Emily to make his new restaurant business a success. Calling him boss and being in close proximity to him is purely a coincidental bonus. After all, over the years, there'd been a time or two when their chemistry nearly combusted.

There is just one obstacle to his grand plan.

Emily has firm plans to follow to make her own career a success, and they don't involve any entanglements with Wes. No siree. The last thing she needs is to add sleeping with her boss to the equation.

Wes, on the other hand, is betting on the fact that he thinks she could use a distraction —in the shape of him. Surely, all he needs to do is throw in a little persuasion to ensure she doesn't get away a third time…

EMILY

"I completely skipped the gym today and opted for a bagel with cream cheese," I say to Sadie, my best friend since childhood. I'm balancing my cell phone under my ear, my heels pattering on the sidewalk.

"Good choice, Ems. I stuck to a donut even though I have to fit into a wedding dress next week, and I'm not at all sorry." I can hear her smiling, as everything to her is positive and peachy lately. That's what happens when you fall in love and the guy who loves you in return wants to literally give you everything—and Logan Jax can and does.

"We should go get cupcakes later after a little retail therapy." I'm busy looking at the numbers on the doors I pass. In the background, the sound of taxis on the Chicago street whiz by, and in the corner of my eye, I notice the occasional passerby on the sidewalk. It's relatively quiet for a Monday morning in late-August.

"For sure, we can celebrate your new job."

I've spent the past few years living in Boston, working at a company that sold water bottles. Unfortunately (or fortunately), that went bust when the CEO decided to throw a wet t-shirt competition for the interns, complete with photos fit for a pinup calendar. At least he used his brand of water. I took that as my chance to move back to Chicago—my hometown. It's also where my parents are.

My dad is in the consulting business, and my mom is a teacher—both are nearing retirement. My best friend, Sadie, is also in Chicago. I knew being closer to them and a change in scenery was just what I needed while I figured out how to redirect my career—my passion, event planning.

With luck, Sadie's father is a corporate lawyer and has quite a few clients in the hospitality industry, and she mentioned that a new restaurant was looking for a temporary organizer. After speaking on the phone with Charlie, the manager, it seemed like the perfect fit and exactly what I need right now to fill my time.

"I owe you, Sadie. I really need something to enhance my resume while I figure out what the hell to do with my life." Getting laid off from your job really throws a wrench into your plans. I gave myself one week of freaking out, then I would get started on my career path.

I did what any person who enjoys planning would do. I grabbed a bottle of pinot grigio, threw on a comfy sweater dress, then mind mapped and mood boarded the fuck out of this life change. With a clear plan in sight, I decided to start with freelancing. One problem I keep running into is that I need a few more jobs on my resume to show I have diverse experience and know the local market.

"Really, this is a step in the right direction." I beam as I take in the tall building up on my right.

"Listen, Emily, there's something you need to know," Sadie begins, but I'm too distracted with arriving at my destination.

"Found the address," I announce with a cheery tone,

excited. Working on the little details of events is when I am most in my element. From decorations to food to music, everything that makes the scene special. When friends have weddings, baby showers, and birthdays, it's usually me who arranges it all—why not get paid to do just that?

I push the heavy revolving door open to Two Tomatoes. It's been a few years since I've been here. It has undergone a change of ownership and some serious renovations. It's definitely not finished, but I can already tell this place is going to get heavy traction.

"Great, but..." Sadie mentions again, but it's only background noise to me as I step inside and am immediately transported from big-city to a world of chic calmness. I would expect a handsome man to appear and hand me a gin & tonic. The thought causes me to straighten the hem of my tailored beige dress.

My eyes are drawn to the wall of windows looking out onto the river. But that's only the backdrop to the open staircase with iron railings leading to an upstairs sitting area. I admire the space with high ceilings. Exposed brick walls with a tint of red make the place feel industrial, and I could imagine this location packed with young Chicagoans on the weekend or a perfect spot for a private reception. There are so many prospects with a space like this.

Lights are yet to be hung, but I could envision black lamps. There's still plastic wrap over furniture, and the subtle sound of drilling from somewhere in the back hits my ears, along with a mix of indie music.

"Wow, this place looks amazing," I remark to Sadie, ignoring what she just said, still too awestruck to listen.

"See Emily, every cloud has a silver lining. So, don't kill me but—"

I notice someone approach me; it must be Charlie.

"Well, I should go. I'll call you after and we can talk," I quickly tell her before swiping my screen and putting my phone into my tan-colored bag.

My head darts up with a welcoming smile.

"Emily Cates, we meet at last," the guy with chocolate-brown hair says as he approaches me with a welcoming look and offers me a hand to shake. He seems to be late-twenties and the type of guy who religiously downs a few protein shakes a day.

"Indeed, and you must be Charlie?" I ask with piqued interest and a smile on my face.

"Yeah, guilty. Can I get you something to drink?" he asks as he studies me, yet respectfully so.

"No, it's okay."

He waves for me to follow him, and I do.

"I love how the restaurant is turning out." I can imagine from the old photos that the building needed a remodel, but I like how it's taking on a modern feel yet keeping some original aspects of the building.

"Yeah, we're getting there. A few more weeks and the final touches then we'll be ready for the re-opening." He indicates for me to take a seat at the bar, and I go along with his lead.

We both sit and get settled, and I notice how his smile is friendly and easy, yet I can't shake the feeling that something in this place has me slightly on edge. I brush it to the side.

"So, we talked briefly on the phone already and you mentioned you've just moved back to Chicago?"

I nod softly and adjust a charm bracelet on my wrist. "Yeah, I was living in Boston and had a great job as a corporate event planner. Unfortunately, the company got involved in a money-laundering scandal, plus the CEO was having an affair with an intern who won the wet t-shirt contest he threw, so the company couldn't save face. Luckily, I got a good severance package to hold me over while I figure out what I want to do with my life."

"Yeah, I read about it online, a water bottle company, right? Were you working there for long?"

"Since I graduated college. So, two years, and I thought I was getting comfortable, but *bam*, the boss literally screwed us all out of a good job." My humor makes him laugh once.

"And then you came back to the place where you grew up?"

"I grew up in the suburbs. The same place as Sadie. However, suburban life isn't my calling quite yet, so I got a place downtown temporarily."

Charlie leans back in his chair and crosses his arms. "I was once in your shoes when I moved back from college in Indiana, I get it. Well, lucky for us, you happen to be here at the right time."

"Am I? You mentioned that you needed an event planner to help in the coming weeks with a few events and the re-opening."

Charlie taps the bar top with his fingertips. "Yes, we need someone part-time who can finalize details on menus, some minor interior things, and take care of a few small parties. We aren't open to the public, but we're still having a few small events in the private room. Plus, Sadie and Wes's dad would like to have a work event here before the opening."

There it is.

Wes.

I thought I had another week to prepare myself for hearing his name. I'm fifty-fifty on the fence of how I should react to him.

A twinge forms inside me at the sound of Wes's name. I knew it would come up at some point. It just still feels the same every time. It never eases. For the life of me, I never could figure out why, either.

Over the years, Sadie has somehow picked up not to mention her older brother's name around me. The popular jock from high school who turned into a mysterious, hardened, and sexy-as-hell adult. Sadie doesn't know why not to mention his name, or at least I don't think she does, but she sensed long ago that he is an irritating matter to me.

I swallow and push forward. "What's the deal with the former planner?"

"She worked here under the old owners but had to suddenly move out of state due to her husband's new job. We were starting to have interviews, but when Sadie called and recommended you and after talking with you on the phone, it felt like a good fit." He reaches over the bar to grab a bottle of water sitting there.

I feel like it's a compliment, although a tad odd, as it's a big risk to take considering we hadn't met. "Oh? Well, I'm honored. I would love to help, but I have to be honest that I'm contemplating starting my own business when it comes to long-term career."

He scratches the back of his neck. "That's okay. Right now we just desperately need someone part-time for the coming weeks. After that we can re-evaluate if there's enough for a full-time position. What is most important is that we get the re-opening done right. Press and reviewers will be bombarding us, and we have to be ready."

I bring my palm up in agreement. "I totally understand."

"Great. So the question is— will you join the team?" He gives me a hopeful look.

"Wow. You're making this process too easy." I have to grin at this whole situation.

"I'm a laid-back person, so why make it complicated?

And Sadie vouched for you, which is good enough for me. Not to mention, I'm running out of time and need the help." He shrugs a shoulder, and I enjoy his genuine honesty. "Plus, you know the Bay family better than anyone we would interview, so this may be a perfect solution for now."

"I guess." Something inside me cautions, and I still can't pinpoint it. Brushing the thought aside, I decide to make small talk to get to know the man I'll be working with.

"You've always worked in hospitality?" I wonder aloud.

"Yeah, pretty much since college. But I'm excited for this place. A lot of time and investment have gone into it since the building was bought four months ago. I'll be happy when we can finally settle after opening. My wife is eager to start a family." Charlie grins to himself and seems proud of that fact.

"Been married long?"

"Three years. You?" I notice he looks at my vacant ring finger. "Obviously no husband, so is there a boyfriend to pick you up on the late nights?"

I chuckle to myself. "No boyfriend. I'm kind of ready to just figure life out a little and don't need the added distraction. I want to re-establish my bearings now that I'm back in town." I twirl gently on the barstool.

"You sound like you have a strong head on your shoulders. I'm hoping this means that you agree to join the team?" He sounds optimistic with his tone.

I study him for a few seconds, but I don't need long. This is one stop on my roadmap of adulthood. "Sounds like the perfect plan."

Relief hits his face and a wide grin forms. "Great. Well, I already sent you the employment forms by e-mail last night so you had an idea what we would be offering if this meeting worked out. You just need to sign those, and you can start on staff for the interim period."

"Okay, I did have a look, and it all seems fair." More than fair, from what I read.

"Perfect, I guess you could start ASAP?"

I nod in agreement.

"Wes is going to be so relieved that I found someone to take on the event planning," Charlie mentions casually. He looks behind him as the drilling from the construction worker stops in the faint distance.

My body stills then my stomach drops, as if a roller-coaster just swooped down the track. "We-Wes?" I barely stutter out.

Charlie looks at me like I'm crazy. "Yeah, Sadie told you, right?"

I shake my head slowly and struggle to blink.

He now looks at me with a mixture of disbelief and humor. "You know Wes is the new owner of this place?"

The shock flooding through me isn't surprising, but it feels just the same every time I hear his name, as my stomach still sinks and little annoying fireflies jump in my body. I'm a smart woman, and maybe deep down I knew there was this possibility. But this is very much… the confirmation.

I offer Charlie a tight-lipped smile and adjust my position on the chair. I pull the hem of my dress over my knees. It suddenly feels warm in here, or maybe it's the usual flush of heat that hits me at the thought of Weston Bay near me—a throwback to the times I should have known better.

"Sorry, I thought you knew."

"Um, well, I just assumed this was one of his father's clients."

"Ah, yes. I mean, his father's firm did handle the contracts, but he's the owner."

My throat feels dry. "I guess you and I will be working together mostly on everything, since you handle the operational side of things?" I try to get clarification of how deep the hole may be that I just got myself into. Because, as much as I could back out, I know this job is exactly what I need for my portfolio. Wes be damned.

"True, normally that would be the case—"

"But Wes wants to be *very* hands-on for the re-opening. So, you will report to me." The voice from behind me shoots that familiar blast through me, and my heart nearly stops. Wes's smooth voice unintentionally wraps warmth around me, and that's not the effect I want.

Slowly, I turn on my chair to glance over at Wes leaning against the railing at the bottom of the stairs, with his ankles crossed. His look of jeans and a dress shirt with a few buttons open is already taunting me, and his stubbled face is just the right length. God, that hair is still a perfect shade of ash brown. His smug grin can't be missed, and his eyes stare directly at me like he has been waiting for this. The perfect height of sin and the perfect build of trouble.

It's been almost a year since I saw him last, but make no mistake, his smolder hasn't lessened. His eyes catch and hold mine, as if he lasered away any barrier I have around me when it comes to him.

"Weston." I drop his name with no feeling laced in my tone, yet inside me, a swirl of emotions is brewing.

"Why, you sound thrilled to see me." He propels away from the railing and takes a few strides in my direction, the whole time his gray eyes never leaving my own. When he lands in front of me, a subtle cunning look spreads across his face.

The undertone of a warning running strong.

2

WES

Emily glances away from me, and I could swear I see the remnants of a smirk on her face. She's entertained by me, I'm sure.

I nod to Charlie to give us some space, and he gets the hint. I practically begged the man for his help this morning, to ensure Emily wouldn't leave until after she agreed to the job.

"Well, I guess I'll see you tomorrow. It was good to meet you, Emily. I guess… I will leave you two to talk." He looks between us and seems amused with the situation and smiles to himself as he slaps my back for encouragement, which I don't exactly need. Not when it comes to this woman.

"You too." She gives him a gentle smile.

The moment Charlie is out of the picture, I slide into his vacant stool. Emily's eyes shoot my way, and I can tell she's debating what to say. For a second, I soften as her brown eyes connect with my own again. Five minutes ago, from upstairs when she wouldn't notice, I already surveyed her like the trophy she is.

Her hair is honey-colored blond at the perfect length, and those soft features on her face still warm people to her in a heartbeat. Then, of course, today she decides to wear a hot-as-fuck fitted dress that gives the right glimpse of her outline, and those bracelets she wears around her wrists, still one too many. It only triggers my brain to remember how my hands fit around her waist and how her body goes limber around me, but only *just*. Because I was a fool twice.

Now she's here. Exactly where I want her to be.

Emily has been my younger sister's best friend since middle school. They were joined at the hip, especially since Emily is an only child. In a way, we grew up together, although I am a few years older than her. I could never see Emily as a little sister, though—a fact that I have proven several times over.

After graduating from university in Michigan, I used my business skills to prosper in the hospitality industry, working for a company that managed several popular spots in Detroit. But I wanted more, I wanted something of my own, and this place is special compared to the others. The moment I stepped foot into this old restaurant, something resonated in me, and it became a sort of passion project. And it only added to my determination too.

"I take it Sadie didn't give you the memo that I own this place?" I ask as I study her to try and figure out her mood, and I can't help but show my enjoyment to this situation.

"Clearly not." Her answer is direct. She briefly glances away, before looking back at me.

But I've got to call her out on this. We both know what the other has been up to without needing to ask directly. It's the perk of Sadie occasionally mentioning the latest gossip. "I heard you were back. You also must have heard that I was back. In fact, I'm confident you thought, maybe for a second, that this could be my business."

She doesn't flinch but does nibble her bottom lip, as if she's trying to control herself.

"And even with that thought somewhere in your head, you still came here. Am I right?" I challenge her, and her eyes snap to me like she's been caught out.

A scoff escapes her. "I knew you were back in Chicago, but I had no clue that *you* owned this place. I thought it was one of your dad's clients."

I lean back on the stool. "Obviously my sister missed a lot of details. I am my dad's client, or at least when he was practicing law. He's been off the past two months—since he had his heart attack." I say that as normal as possible considering the circumstances of what's transpired the past few months with John Bay, good old Dad.

Her hand reaches forward, as if she wants to touch my arm to comfort me, but she stops halfway. Instead, her hand returns to her side and she smooths her dress.

"I'm happy he's doing better. I saw him briefly the other week with Sadie, and he almost seems fully recovered," she mentions, and I know her kind-hearted spirit is purely genuine.

"Yeah, he's doing well. Heading back to work next week." He still knows how to rub me the wrong way too.

For a moment, we get lost looking at the other. Our usual play.

She smiles to herself. "So, I guess this is us running into one another again." It comes out with a hint of humor.

Scratching my cheek, I have to grin. "It is," I confirm.

"Look, Wes." She hops off the stool and begins to leave. "This is probably a bad idea." Emily walks a few steps before she abruptly stops and turns around. Her look is almost a daggered stare.

"Wait," she holds her palm up. "Did you know Charlie was interviewing me?"

My mouth tugs, as I have no problem admitting the truth. "Charlie phoning you was pure coincidence, I only found out after he spoke with you. I can imagine Sadie didn't know I would be here, but I knew you would be. So yes, I had Charlie do the front work, and here we are. Didn't think you would show if you had the idea that you would be calling me boss."

She grunts a laugh as she brings her hands to her hips. "I am *not* calling you boss." She lets out an audible exhale and contemplates what to say as her fingers tap her hipbone, drawing me in.

"But you still agree to work here?"

Her head rolls to the side. "Wes," she draws out my name, as if she's still undecided.

Instantly, I stand up and grab her arm, the surge of electricity between us ignited yet again, as it always happens when we're around one another. We've been here before. I feel her still under my touch as we both peer down to my hand on her arm, aware that we're in physical contact.

Quickly, I interject. "It's got to be you."

Our eyes meet again, and her lids blink several times. I see the confusion in her eyes, but it only adds to the fuel of how beautiful she looks today.

For a moment, I would swear her lips part open to say something profound, but she runs her tongue to the corner of her mouth, which doesn't help my imagination or memory, and by the feeling of my dick hardening, then I may enter crisis mode soon. She has the perfect mouth to kiss, but I can't think about that now, as I need my A-game to make this work.

Emily gives me the once-over before reluctantly returning

to her chair. "Enlighten me—why in the world does it need to be me?"

I hold a finger up, indicating for her to wait. I pull out my phone from my pocket and swipe my screen until I reach an email, then show her the screen which has the list of who is coming to the opening.

She looks and then her mouth gapes open. "Wow, how did you manage that invite list? Those are some big names, and those bloggers aren't half bad either. If you get in their good books then you're set."

I completely ignore her question, because she doesn't need to hear how my charm persuaded some of that guest list. I tuck my phone back in my pocket. "I really do need someone to make the opening run smoothly. Is it really that bad if we have to work together? I know how you like a challenge." I rub the stubble on my chin as I study her.

Her cheeks raise slightly which tells me she's trying to withhold a smile. "I just don't think you as *the challenge* is a good idea. We've been doing so well avoiding one another; why ruin a good streak?"

I grin at her logic and move my upper body slightly forward, enough that her perfume invades my senses, the same as always, subtle with a hint of cinnamon.

"You and I are going to face each other a lot. I mean, next weekend alone, Sadie is upgrading that big rock on her finger to a wedding ring. Consider this practice." No hypotheticals. Emily is the maid of honor. I'm Sadie's brother. I mean, it's a guarantee that we will be forced to interact.

She shakes her head and seems slightly entertained. "Wes." It's her warning purr. The sound I've heard a few times, the battle call that my dick can't ignore.

"Emily." I return the tone and let my fingers gently graze

her arm that's resting on the bar top, as if her body is part of my property.

"Working together is a horrible idea." She looks up toward the ceiling with a grin, but to my surprise, she doesn't jerk her arm away from my touch.

"It's really not. But do you really want to pass up the opportunity? I mean, everyone is eyeing this as the opening of the year. It'll put you on the map."

Now she gives me that coy smile that makes me weak every time. "Ooh, someone is a little brash these days. That was never your style, so don't start it now."

And she's right. Beginning with high school, when I was the varsity football player, until now, as the high-roller property investor, I've never let success get to me.

"Maybe so, but I've changed. I'm not the same guy as before." I'm more determined, persuasive, and I know exactly what I want.

Her head retreats back slightly. "Now I'm intrigued." I love the way she just gave me a flirty grin there.

"I just mean that if we both know what's at stake professionally here, we both could benefit from a successful opening, career-wise, obviously."

"True but—"

I squeeze her arm to assure her. "I promise I'll be professional the entire time."

She hesitates and bites her lip again, a nervous habit that I recognize. "Okay."

Relief hits me that this isn't going to be a longer debate, and a victorious smile spreads across my face.

"Perfect. I have no doubt you will do a good job."

She holds her long finger up. "A *great* job," she corrects me.

"You will do a great job," I confirm with a grin.

A short pause enters our conversation, and maybe we both get lost in the thought that we're both in the same city at the same time and now thrown together. The factors that were always missing before in our alchemy as two people who can't pinpoint a title of what they are.

"I mean it, Professional Wes, all the way," she nearly whispers, her eyes not blinking.

"Sure."

It's a good few beats again before she breaks our piercing gaze. "You are making quite a name of yourself." I swear I can hear a hint of pride in her voice.

"Maybe." I play modest, but I know at age twenty-eight that I *am* doing well. Back in Detroit, I found myself mentioned in a few local magazines, singing my praises for the venues I managed. When I became an investor, my name kept growing. I now have enough money in my bank account to be more than comfortable.

"It's a beautiful place here. I actually can't believe this is all you." She gently smiles as she looks around.

"Thanks. Not quite finished, and construction was a pain. I'll most definitely rely on the chef and Charlie to make this work… and *you*, obviously."

The corners of her mouth twist at my statement.

"And the name of the restaurant?" she asks, curious.

I scratch my cheek and grin. "Two Tomatoes is not the name we're keeping. It has a new name."

"Yeah, it doesn't sound like you. So, what's the new name?"

"Jupiter."

She instantly freezes and takes in my words. She gulps, even. Maybe because it means something to her. Before she thinks too deeply, I correct any notion. "The marketing guys I work with gave me a list of names, and Jupiter was on it. It sets a good tone, and someone once mentioned to me that Jupiter has the longest nights, and that's when exciting things happen," I remind her casually.

She looks away before she nearly blushes but moves past my quip. "I thought I had another week before I would see you."

I cross my arms and admire her truth. "Were you mentally preparing?" She doesn't answer. "It's better this way."

Her head tilts to the side. "Why is that?"

Placing my hands on each side of her, one on the chair and the other on the bar top, I lean into her personal space, causing her breath to catch.

"Because I need you to agree to work here before the wedding so you can't back down, because I know you would say no after what I have planned for you this weekend." I retreat back slightly with a confident look, my lips at a perfect distance to nip the corner of her mouth if I wanted. The mouth that has parted open slightly from my words.

I hope her blank look is a sign that she's imagining the things I'll do to her—and fuck me, I hope she is calculating which black lace panties to wear too.

"I'm in trouble, aren't I?" She swallows, and I love how it comes out a flirty yet serious whisper.

I lick my lips at her statement because she knows me too well. "Maybe." I turn casual. "Stay for lunch?"

She shakes her head slowly and instead grabs her purse. "Absolutely not. I will see you tomorrow for *Professional* Wes." The corner of her mouth slants up.

"Absolutely," I assure her. "And I know we're stretching it with timing for the opening and adding my dad's event to the mix." Plus, I have a point to prove to the old man.

"We'll make it work. I already have some ideas."

My parents are both lawyers, and although our childhood

was filled with them working more hours than a normal person should, they gave us a good life—and quite often an unhealthy dose of career pressure too.

I stand at the same time as her and we bump into one another, which causes us both to freeze. I notice in our pause that she takes a deep inhale, as if she's remembering my scent. I place my hand on her arm to steady her, and it takes all my restraint not to pull her closer.

She looks up at me. "Tomorrow." She gulps. "I'll see you tomorrow."

I can only nod once before she dashes off, as if she needs to escape me.

The clearing of a throat breaks my attention on Emily's every step out of my restaurant, and I turn to see Charlie heading behind the bar.

"Contractor says he'll be finished by Wednesday, and the new dishes arrived. Still haven't received the electrician's confirmation that he can come to hang the lighting by the end of the week."

I break my thought. "Nothing new then. I'll chase him this afternoon." I can't wait for all this logistical stuff to be over with. I just want to focus on menus and having actual people coming to eat here. Pulling my phone out, I type myself a reminder to check about the beer delivery.

"There some kind of a story there between you two?" Charlie asks, and I watch him searching for something on the counter. I know he means Emily.

"A story? Not quite. A beginning to a story, yeah." Because that's as far as we ever got, and now we need our ending. My mind goes in circles some days at the thought of *what if.*

She's the memory that surfaces every time a date with someone else fails. Every time I need a moment to breathe.

Every time I feel the need to connect with someone who believes in me, even when she and I never got more of what we may have wanted.

When Sadie mentioned that Emily moved back, it was a no-brainer that I should reach out, but fate stepped in, and I knew this could be our fresh start.

"She is coming back, right? Because we do legit need her," he reminds me, as we have a lot to do, and neither one of us are in the mood to choose flowers or figure out the feng shui of furniture.

"She is."

Charlie gets to work on opening a box. "What made her agree?"

"I said I would be Professional Wes." I give wide eyes to Charlie who laughs.

"That's the biggest lie of the century."

And don't I know it.

I place both hands on the bar and lean in. "It is. But I wasn't going to tell her that I plan on pursuing the hell out of her. No way am I letting her get away a third time."

EMILY

Leaning against the doorframe of Sadie's place, I have a cheap bottle of Chardonnay hanging from one hand. She looks up to find my dismayed grimace, while my pale-pink nails on my other hand tap the frame of the door. She instantly knows what—actually, *who*—brought this moment of frustration on. The moment Sadie sees me, she gives me a pained smile as she finishes putting her brownish-red hair up in a messy bun.

With the door fully open, I barge past Sadie into her penthouse, heading straight for the kitchen. Not that she even cares about those things, but she ended up with a fiancé who came with a castle in the sky. With Logan still working his usual long hours, Sadie took advantage of some much-needed time off to get ready for the wedding.

Stationing myself at the kitchen island, I get to work on peeling the foil off the bottle.

"Forgot to mention a *mucho* minor detail." My brows arch up as I look at Sadie who seems equal parts scared of my wrath and humored by me.

She heads to the cupboard to pull two glasses out. "I didn't know he would be there, honestly," she protests.

"*Really?* You didn't think that your brother who owns the place would show up?" I'm full of disbelief.

"I thought Charlie does all the managing and operational stuff. Wes is so busy meeting with suppliers and still goes back to Detroit a lot that I just thought he wouldn't involve himself in the day-to-day operations."

She slides the wine tumbler my way.

"Guess again. *He is.*" I pour myself a glass of vino to the rim.

Sadie seems to be studying me and bites her lip, trying to figure out what to say. She bites the bullet. "Look, I maybe also didn't mention it because I didn't want you to not consider the job. I don't know what happened between you two, but obviously we are all adults, so this isn't a big deal, right?" She sounds hopeful.

Ahh, being mature sucks sometimes. "You're right." I take a chug of wine to calm my nerves.

Because, truthfully, the idea of being in close proximity to Wes the next few weeks does a lot to me on all fronts. I just can't figure out what is more overpowering inside me. The way Wes still looks at me, a sort of sweltering heat in his eyes that makes my body struggle not to respond. Or the raging emotion in me because of lost chances.

"Did you sleep with him?" she blurts out.

I stop mid-swallow and turn it into a mouthful as I take in the question from my best friend. She has never asked for details of why I get so bothered by her brother, and I'll assume she doesn't notice how hot I get at the mention of his name too.

It wasn't always this way. In high school, we were all fine. Then freshman year of college and *bam*, the axis of the earth changed for me. Since then, I only tune in occasionally when Sadie talks about Wes. They're close enough, but he luckily doesn't come up in conversation too often.

The clearing of a throat reminds me that Sadie is waiting patiently for my answer. She's never asked but maybe always wondered.

I look to her. "No… we didn't." Kind of a lie, but kind of true too.

Sadie studies me as she takes a sip of her wine. "Hmm, you don't sound disgusted by the thought either."

My eyes bug out at her in surprise before shaking my head in utter annoyance.

"Anyhow, it's good that you two have never hooked up or anything," she mentions, and for some reason it disappoints me.

"Oh?" I want to know why, as if this is a factor for the future. *Crazy.*

"I mean, it could get kind of awkward. Could you imagine what my wedding would be like if you two had hooked up at some point?" She laughs slightly to herself while I finish off the dry white in my hand. "What if I would have to choose sides. I would be part of a custody agreement between my friend and brother. That would not be cool," she continues on, and I wish the bottle of wine would pour itself.

"Listen, Sadie, let's just focus on your upcoming nuptials —the ones that I wasn't allowed to plan." I pretend to be annoyed at that fact.

Sadie grins at me. "I wish you could have, but the venue was really strict about using their own on-site planner." Sadie is getting married at the place where she met Logan, a fancy members-only club overlooking the lake.

"It's okay. I guess it means I can actually enjoy the wedding like a guest," I reassure her with a smile.

"And since you're working for Wes then it won't be an issue anymore that you run into one another at my small, *intimate* wedding." She flashes her eyes at me.

I drag the bottle of wine my way. "Guess so. So tell me what kind of things your dad likes. Charlie mentioned he's having a small dinner for his work soon."

"Sure, let me get us some snacks and then we can chat," Sadie mentions as she heads to the fridge.

A few minutes later, she has a cheese and cracker plate out for us. Okay, we definitely should get points for being sophisticated mid-twenty-year-olds.

We talk about her dad's big return to work and his plan to celebrate. She tells me what food her parents enjoy, what flowers her mother likes, and maybe what music to play. I throw in a few of my ideas to see if Sadie likes them. Perhaps a specialty drink that reflects her father's personality. Tables dressed formally with a somewhat healthy menu.

"Love these ideas." She leans against the back of the sofa, and Sadie seems happy as she tucks her feet under her knees. "You know, at my wedding you should dance with Cole. I bet you and him would hit it off."

Cole is her fiancé's best friend and is easy on the eyes. Honestly, a full package, complete with suit and a thick checkbook. But he isn't… well, I don't know, my type.

I answer as neutrally as possible. "I'll consider it, but I think Ruby wouldn't be thrilled." She's our other friend who I feel has an interest in the man.

"Probably." Sadie's face spreads into a beaming smile. "Eee! I'm so excited for the big day."

"You should be. Logan is crazy about you, and by this time next week, he'll be your husband." I interlink our arms, and we both lean against the couch. "And I have never seen you so happy."

"I am. He's even getting along with my brother, so the reception dinner should be a breeze. Since we talked about Wes and now he's your boss then I will assume it won't be a problem if we all grace the same table."

"Let's not call him my boss, and I knew you were going to place us at the same table anyhow."

"But he *is* kind of your boss," she teases me and gives me a side glance.

I can only shake my head.

What am I doing?

————

THE NEXT MORNING, I down a green smoothie that I made for breakfast. I look around my small, simple apartment. It still needs some character thrown in. Other than mood boards and post-it notes, there aren't many personal touches. Maybe it's because I don't want to get too comfortable, as I am hoping to find something more permanent, or it could very well be that planning everyone else's celebrations means I never get around to the needs of my own space. And for now, I'm okay with that.

After throwing on a simple black dress paired with aqua-blue accessories, I debate wearing my hair up or down. Catching a glimpse of myself in the mirror, I know my decision to leave my hair down is because it will drive Wes crazy —it did in the past, anyways.

A deep yoga breath doesn't do the trick to send me on my merry way, but I persevere and make my way to the restaurant. Luck was on my side, when I arrived and saw that Wes had not arrived yet. Instead, Charlie and I walked through the building, and I ran some ideas of how to lay out the private room for a few small events coming up.

Since the opening is in a few weeks, I suggested we treat a few of the smaller events as soft opening testers. This would allow us to try different menus with some of the private parties and test the waters for the big event.

Walking through the restaurant, Charlie introduced me to chef Reggie and a few waiters who are in to unpack dishes. Everyone seems pretty laid-back. There's a nice vibe to the place.

As we walk away from the kitchen, Charlie clears his throat. "Can I ask something?"

"Sure." I smile curiously.

"It's not going to be a problem, right? I mean… well… I picked up on some vibes." He gives me a strained look and I realize he means Wes and me.

"Oh." I nearly frown. "True. Wes and I are no strangers, but it's not an issue." *I hope.*

Charlie looks relieved yet has an almost grin, as if something is funny. "Oh, good, because I don't enjoy workplace drama, especially when the boss is involved."

"Trust me. You have nothing to worry about." Because I will stay strong.

I like how Charlie seems mellow, just a general good guy. I would hate to cause him stress, actually.

"Hey, I never asked. When you interviewed me, you mentioned you've always worked in hospitality, but was it always here?"

"No, but Wes and I knew one another in college, so I think I got points during the interview process," he replies as he wipes the bar top with a fresh rag.

"You went to college in Indiana, though, right?"

"True, but I met Wes at… You know what, I'll leave that story for another day." There seems to be something that makes him smile to himself, and my curiosity is piqued, but I decide to focus on work instead.

After an hour of looking at sample menus and discussing the budget I've been given, Charlie and I sit at the bar as I take notes. When he tilts his head up, I know he's nodding to someone behind me. My body's quickening pulse tells me that Wes has arrived.

"Morning, you two," Wes greets us as he circles around the bar. Today, his gray button-down shirt with a slight sheen only enhances his eyes. *Just great.* He gives me a knowing smile as he grabs himself a bottle of water from the fridge.

"No good morning for your boss?"

"Is this how it's going to go every day?" I respond, due to his efforts to already taunt me. I cross my arms and give him a stern eye. "Why, good morning, Weston. I do hope you have a wonderful day." I'm over the top.

It makes his smile widen. "Now there's the spirit. So, did Charlie show you around and set you up with everything to get started?" He drinks from his bottle.

"Yep, she's ready to go," Charlie replies.

"Great. So, I'll just leave everything to you, Emmy?" Wes stops mid-drink when he realizes he said my nickname, the one only he calls me.

Our eyes catch briefly, and after a pause only we would notice, I continue. "Yeah, sure."

"Still have the meeting with the supplier?" Charlie asks.

"Yeah, that's today. Then we can finalize the menu with Reggie. A shame the supplier is located outside the city, though. To western Illinois of all places," Wes explains as he rolls up his sleeves, and I notice his watch. Something sexy about a man who wears a good watch… in general, I mean. *Men in general. Not Wes.*

"That's a bit of a trek. I guess you'll both be gone most of the day," I comment as I look between them.

Charlie looks awkwardly up from his phone then glances between Wes and me as Wes lets a grunted laugh escape.

"Why, yes. *You* and I will be gone for most of the day." Wes flashes me a sneaky look.

I look between both men, and Charlie must pick up on the odd vibe in the room.

"I need to stay here and train the new staff." Charlie shrugs his shoulders before rolling off his stool and heading toward the kitchen.

Turning my attention to Wes, I roll my eyes and take a breath to try and relax. This is no big deal. I knew something like this would happen. Eye on the prize—a solid resume.

"Fine then. I guess we're going to the supplier." I tap my nails on the bar top.

"Yep." He pops the P with his lips. "You and me."

———

FIVE MINUTES LATER, I'm strapping myself into the front seat of his SUV as he puts the address in the GPS. When that feminine voice of the navigation informs us the time to destination is ninety minutes, I mentally calculate in my head the time there, an hour or two with the supplier, then two hours back since we'll hit traffic.

Fuck. This is going to turn into a long day.

"Want to pick the music?" he offers.

"Sure." I grab my phone from my bag and scroll my playlists before picking a mix of acoustic folk and setting it on the Bluetooth.

When I glance up, we are already on our merry way.

"There's something for you on the back seat," he tells me as he drives, and it spikes my curiosity.

Looking over my shoulder, a wide smile spreads on my face as I grab the white bag. "Since when is Olly O's in the city?" I look into the bag filled with donuts from our hometown bakery.

"They apparently opened up a location six months ago. Thought we could use some road-trip snacks."

I notice my favorite maple-glazed donut in the bag. "You knew you would be dragging me across the state and didn't think to warn me. Instead, you brought supplies to try and butter me up?"

He turns on a wicked grin with a wink. "Exactly."

"Fine, but if you misbehave then I am biting into your cruller with no remorse," I counter before taking a bite into my maple-glazed treat.

"I never misbehave… unless you're around."

A sound escapes me as I roll my eyes and move us past his attempt to remind me of another time. "So, what should I expect from the supplier?"

"Olive Owl is a farm halfway between here and Lake Galena. The owners are friends of Cole and Logan. The farm has olive oil, jams, special cheeses, but it's actually their pumpkins and lettuce that I'm after. They are also trying their hand at wine too. It's a great-looking spot. A lot of people have weddings there. Anyhow, I want to source local stuff from here in Illinois so thought I would give these people a try. It's a family business."

I get overly excited, because he's not wrong, local supplies are always the best for events. "I love pumpkins, and that's great that you want to try and keep things local. But I'm still on to you."

He quickly glances over at me with a confused face.

I have to laugh. "Pretty sure that I'm not needed for this little rendezvous. You don't really need me to come along."

"Maybe I need your insight on pumpkins, but anyway, I'm confident this won't be a wasted trip," he assures me as he changes lanes.

"Right," I confirm softly, and I feel the faint twitch of a smile on my lips.

"Guess we're driving by our hometown out in the burbs."

His choice of words makes me laugh. "Yeah, because you are such a city boy now."

Wes glances over at me. "Says the one who moved to the city. I don't exactly see you living the suburban dream."

"I'm only twenty-five, I'm supposed to want to live the city life." I shrug.

A long, odd silence graces the car as only music plays, and it feels like minutes.

Until he says, "Actually, I was thinking we could grab dinner on the way back, to break up the drive a bit."

"Is this what Professional Wes would normally do with a colleague?" I have to wonder or tease, I don't know. But this weird ease around him is creeping up. It happens every time without fail. As if nothing ever happened or time hasn't passed. It's natural, but nonetheless scary, because we can so easily fall back into what there was before.

"Yes. Professional Wes doesn't let his employees starve, and can we stop talking in the third person?"

"Maybe… I'll consider it."

I notice the faint lines of a winning smirk form on his face.

We manage to talk occasionally about random things that signs on the highway trigger us to talk about. New places, new restaurants. For a moment, I remember those few times around him, and I glance at him, wondering if it ever crosses his mind the way it does mine.

It's when we leave suburban Chicago and begin to drive through the flat land of green corn with yellow tips that he confirms what I wondered.

"So, this is the first time we're in a car together since…"

I immediately turn my attention to him, slightly shocked he's bringing it up so boldly.

The corners of his mouth tug. "Since, well, the night you began to hate me."

Our eyes briefly connect with a similar look of blazing recognition.

4

WES

I abruptly pull the car to the side of the road. There have only been a few trucks passing us for the last ten minutes, plus a few cars with Iowa license plates, so this move isn't crazy. Shoving the car into park, I turn the music down and adjust my body to face her.

"One of us has to bring it up," I tell her rather firmly.

She scoffs at my sentence, and Emily's eyes surge with annoyance. She attempts to open her door but struggles as the child lock prevents her from escaping.

"What the hell, Wes? I don't hate you, but I definitely don't want to be locked in a small space with you having this conversation. Ugh. Let me out." She searches for the unlock button, and the irritation she has for me is reiterated by the jabbing of her finger on the button.

"You're just going to leave?" The corner of my mouth hitches up as I watch her, and honestly, I am quite entertained.

"No, I need air. I need space. I need to not look at you for one second so I can think clearly."

"You're not looking at me," I remind her, and she growls at my response.

As she clicks her seatbelt free, I gently and with caution touch her arm.

"Look at me," I request.

Slowly her head turns to my direction.

"Let's talk, Emmy."

"You think kidnapping me is the way to have that talk?" Her brows arch up, yet I see she's calming down.

I smile softly. "I'm not kidnapping you." I hit the unlock button with my other hand to prove the point. "See?" I give her knowing eyes. "You are free to go… but I know you don't want to."

"And why is that?" She's challenging me, her eyes never blinking.

My hand touching her arm travels up until my fingers graze the edges of her soft, thick hair that I play with by wrapping around my finger. The action makes her lips part, almost a surrender.

"Because if we're going to have any kind of relationship —professional or not—then we need to bury the hatchet."

"Professional relationship! Only professional relation-ship," she reminds me as she moves away and lets her back sink against the seat.

I lick my lips at how difficult she's being. I've never seen her like this. Sure, she is definitely a strong and domineering personality, but not stiff or prickly.

"Want to talk about it? We've avoided this discussion for years."

She looks at me, nibbles her lip, and I can see she's in deep thought.

"And *now,* on my first day, you want to talk about it? You are a horrible boss." She crosses her arms, and I can't figure out if she's truly pissed or feeling the same as me—it's time.

"I'm your temporary boss, and I will be the best boss you ever had, trust me. Now let's talk."

"Don't we have a supplier to see?" She's trying to tear us away from the topic.

"We have time," I say as I adjust the temperature control then lean back in my seat.

"Not for this, we don't." She huffs.

I wait for her to start, and meanwhile, my memory recalls how this all began. Emily was eighteen, and I was heading into my final year of college. It was the summer, and Sadie was with my parents on a graduation trip to San Francisco.

———

SITTING OUTSIDE, I stare at the fire in the pit in the backyard with a beer bottle in hand. A few of my old buddies just left after a BBQ, and I decided to just stay outside and relax. The sound of crickets is soothing, and the sky is clear tonight.

"Hey, you are here." Emily's voice from behind me catches me off guard, as I wasn't expecting her. I turn around and watch her walking my way before she plants herself next to me on the bench swing.

"Yeah, what are you doing here?"

"What am I doing here? What are you doing here?" She glances at me, and I swear her eyes give me a once-over before she throws me a bag of marshmallows that she must have found in the kitchen.

"You mean my parents' house?" I remind her as I look at the fire crackling under the night sky.

"You're not supposed to be here is what I mean. It's the whole reason your folks asked if I could check on the mail

and feed the cat while they're away. It's only when I noticed your car in the garage that I figured I should refrain from calling the cops."

I lean back against the seat and study her. I haven't seen her since Sadie's graduation party and that was only briefly for a few minutes.

Her jean shorts and loose off-the-shoulder pink top only add to the distraction of her long, smooth legs and sun-kissed skin that nearly shimmers with the light of the fire illuminating her. I've always noticed her, but I would shut those thoughts off in an instant, as I had the idea it wasn't appropriate. However, Emily is no longer the sweet friend of my kid sister. She's eighteen and off to college in a few weeks.

We stare at one another, and the reflection of firelight on her face softens her features.

"Everything okay? Nobody knows you're here." Her warm eyes hold me, and I hear the concern in her voice.

"Just needed some quiet before heading into the final stretch." I nudge her arm with mine.

"I can imagine. Still plan on being an entrepreneur?" she asks with interest, maybe even a hint of excitement for me.

I ended up studying business development, ruining my parents' hopes that I would follow in their steps and become a lawyer.

"Yeah... and actually, I'm excited to start all of that. I've been brainstorming ideas already. You? Excited for college?" I ask as I take a sip from my beer. She's heading to Boston for her undergrad.

"Sure, business administration, here I come." She doesn't sound enthused.

"You'll figure it out."

"Sounds like you already have."

I reflect on her sentence. "Maybe true." In my head I

imagine discussing business plans and delegating tasks to employees. King of my own fucking castle. But I have to graduate first, and truthfully, that isn't a breeze. I'm barely hanging on grade-wise. I got sidetracked and didn't keep my head in the books.

But I look at her and anything about business or college leaves my mind. She stares at me with doe eyes and a permanent half-smile.

"I guess housesitting has been cancelled for me since you're here. You probably want some peace too, so I'll go—"

I stop her by touching her arm as she begins to move. "Stay. I don't need peace from you."

Actually, she always makes the moment easy. We've always talked every time we would run into each other. Over spring break, we ran into one another when she was staying over for a movie night with Sadie. We talked for an hour while Sadie was asleep on the couch. We laughed like it was the most natural thing. I couldn't stop thinking that I just wanted to touch her, keep laughing with her. Kiss her... But I didn't kiss her, didn't even touch her. I carefully stayed behind my barrier of the kitchen island.

I can see her subtle smile form from my answer as she eases back onto the bench, and my foot on the ground helps give us momentum to swing gently.

She grabs my beer bottle, but I hold it firm so she can't take it, with my eyes fixed on hers. "You drove here?" I give her an inquisitive look, as she knows better.

She sighs, "True," and drops her hand from the bottle. "Now pass me the fluffy goodness." She grabs the bag of marshmallows.

"That I can agree to."

Two minutes later, we're roasting marshmallows and both seem to enjoy the scene.

"Such a great night out. I wish we didn't live in the suburbs and instead were somewhere in the middle of nowhere. Apparently you can see a few planets tonight."

I give her side-eye. "Really? You don't strike me as the geeky type."

She playfully swats my arm. "That's not geeky. Space and planets are actually super interesting to study. Take, for instance, Jupiter—it has the shortest days of any planet. That's kind of cool since nights are always more magical."

"Huh, is this why you didn't go to prom? Do you secretly prefer planets and space to partying with your people?" I remember Sadie mentioning it to me, and I felt it was a loss that Emily didn't dress up or have some guy waiting for her with a corsage. But then I grinned when I learned it was her independent decision.

She looks at me, taken aback. "No! I didn't go because I was rebelling against the cause." Her defensiveness is cute.

"What cause would that be?"

"Molly Jay taking over the prom committee and totally ignoring all my ideas." She smirks to herself proudly.

"So, you missed the whole thing?"

"Yep. Which is fine, as I wasn't really feeling the options for dates. The pool of toads in my year ran mighty big." She takes a big bite of the white fluff.

"You don't sound like you regret it."

"Nope. Not at all."

She licks her lips, and I imagine the taste of sugar coating her flesh. Suddenly I feel like this night may become a challenge of self-control.

"You went to your prom. Everyone was surprised you didn't get named prom king." She gives me a mischievous look. "You looked good."

I chuckle slightly and lean back. "Feels so long ago.

College is a different world. Stay away from the guys. They'll be swarming to you, but there's not a single one worthy."

"Why do you say that?"

"Because you'll make someone really happy one day. It's in your nature to please and care for people. But don't romance them, let them romance you. They should work for it. You deserve no less."

"Is that why you don't have a girlfriend lately? Because I'm positive you deserve someone." I like how she has so much confidence in me, considering she had a ringside seat to all my bad decisions in high school and on college breaks when it came to girls.

I look at her and notice the morsel of marshmallow on the corner of her lip. I reach out and let my thumb stroke the milky soft skin of her cheek.

"You have no idea," I tell her softly, reminding myself that I need to be a gentleman. But the reminder in my brain is ignored when I notice her eyes staring at my mouth.

I lean in a few inches to test the waters, to feel if I would scare her away, but her eyes close, as if she's waiting for me.

But tonight is different. We have our opportunity.

Noticing her breath picking up, I have my confirmation. Closing in on her mouth with my own, I softly kiss the corner of her lips. Her audible breath shows me she doesn't mind this in the least.

"You taste so sweet," I murmur against her skin as my hand moves to tangle in her hair.

"Don't stop," she rasps.

My lips meet hers and they're warm and firm. I can tell she wants me to lead. I take more from her by slipping my tongue inside her mouth, and that's when she returns my movements with mirroring strokes. The sticks of marshmallow in our hands fall to the ground before our hands find each other's faces to frame.

We kiss deeper, and fuck, I want to bring her closer to me.

Parting with foreheads touching, we try to catch a breath.

"I've always wanted you to do that," she hums, and I can hear the smile in her words.

"Me too."

———

LOOKING BACK at Emily and I know she's just remembered the same moment.

"We had a good few days." She sighs and turns away from me.

"We did," I confirm, and a subtle hint of a smile tries to break on my face, but it can't.

After the first night of kissing her by the fire, holding her close and giving her my sweater to keep her warm, our few days progressed. *"Just you watch, Weston Bay. You will get everything you want one day,"* she would always remind me as her arms wrapped around my neck, because she wanted to hear about every business idea I had in my head, then she'd make these brainstorm maps on paper with different-colored pens to prove that she believed in my ideas.

During those days, I would hold her hand like she was mine and kiss her as if time didn't matter.

One kiss led to many. Before long, kisses led to taking it further. We were doing everything together. Everything except the one thing I wanted so desperately.

"I just don't understand," she says faintly, still avoiding my gaze.

Our timeline of memories is exactly on the same schedule. We're both thinking about the time that changed us—and not the way I would have liked.

We were in the back of my car, hot and heavy, her breathy kisses driving me crazy. Then she stopped me with her hand, and with such conviction in her voice, she said, *"I want to do everything with you. I want my first time to be with you."*

I wanted all of her. I wanted what she was offering. I wanted to be the guy who was her first. I sure as hell didn't want another guy to have the honors.

Yet I couldn't be that guy.

"I didn't understand. I still don't," she mentions before getting her door open and hopping out of the car.

Instantly, I get out and circle the car, remembering that I dropped her off at home that night, and we haven't spoken about this until now.

I find her leaning against the door with arms crossed as I approach her and step into her space. She doesn't push or move away. Instead, she remains firm in her stance.

Emily swallows. "You and I did a lot of things, but then you just…" She tries to turn away.

"Look at me." I'm firm, and reluctantly her eyes dart back. "What? We kissed, you came all over my fingers, my mouth, but when you said you wanted me to be your first, then I said no."

She blinks then tries to move away again with a sigh.

"Look at me," I grind out the demand again. "You have this uncanny ability to make me become a respectable human around you. You were mad at me, I get it. But you didn't deserve to have your first time in the back of my car with me leaving the next day to live thousands of miles away from you."

Fuck no, she deserved a grand gesture and the warmth

and privacy of a bed. Someone who would take her to dinner the next day and do it all over again with her.

She doesn't answer so I reach out and grab her shoulder, trying to encourage her to return back to my direction.

"So very noble of you," she bluntly tells me, and it's filled with cynicism.

I shake my head slightly and step back.

"Stop! Listen, I know it was confusing and frustrating, but I did what I thought was the right thing, and besides, in the grand scheme of things, that isn't what you're annoyed about." My voice hitches slightly due to irritation.

Her jaw drops low in surprise at what I just said. Truthfully, egging her on in this conversation wasn't my plan, but she needs a reminder.

I step closer to her again, and it causes her to back against the door, trapped between me and the car.

"Because maybe it's what happened a year ago that really has you bothered," I remind her with wide eyes about the second missed opportunity between us.

She rolls her own eyes as her hand finds her hip. "A repeat brought on by tainted orange juice."

"Sure, sweetheart, if that's what you would like to think. We both know you wanted it as much as me."

"You're getting a little brave with the confidence, claiming that you aren't responsible for our blunder number two."

I place my arm against the door near her head and lean in, causing her to stiffen. A satisfied smirk forms on my mouth. "That's because it won't be our last."

5

EMILY

Gently I shake my head in disbelief at his ludicrous notion, but deep within me the fear that he's right creeps up.

"You want to hash that out too? You kissed me," I snipe the reminder, pointing a finger at him.

"*Oh*, did I? I think that's up for debate. But I don't care who initiated it, it was fucking good." Does his devilishly sexy grin ever fade?

I keep the urge to also smile controlled, and instead I clear my throat.

The sound of cars passing reminds me that we're standing on the side of the road as our eyes meet for a silent recognition. My head spins from the memory.

———

"One tequila and that's it," I tell Ruby who flashes her eyes at me with pure trouble and brushes her jet-black hair behind her shoulder. We went to high school together until she went away to boarding school. I'm only back to Chicago

for a quick visit, and after lunch with my parents out in the suburbs, Ruby's invite to check out a new club downtown seemed like some excitement for the weekend.

Swaying my hips to a 90s throwback song, I quickly down the tequila as Ruby dances next to me. No, I take that back, she isn't dancing. She's putting on a full show for the guy she has been checking out for the last three minutes from across the dance floor.

"No more tequila. I'll be sticking to vodka and orange juice," I try to speak to her over the loud music.

"Oh, come on, Emily, one more tequila."

I shake my head at her as I keep dancing, completely aware that my blue dress shows enough skin to make me question my motives for this evening, but I got the dress on sale and it looks good on me.

She nudges my arm and leans in. "Hey, isn't that Sadie's brother?"

My eyes follow her line of sight, and a nervous energy hits me as soon as I see Wes talking with the guy Ruby had just been staring at. Lo and behold, of all the places in the world, there he is. I'm not drunk and only on the verge of tipsy, which means I'm too sober for this.

"I, uh, yeah. That's Wes," I confirm and stop dancing. "You know, I think I need that drink now. Want something?"

"Yeah, Wes's friend." She indicates her head across the room.

"Ruby, come on." I grab her arm and drag us through the busy dancefloor to the bar. My eyes stay focused on getting the bartender's attention, and I try to avoid the challenge of not glancing over in Wes's direction. Unfortunately, I've already been distracted by his dark shirt that accentuates his physique—his biceps and tapered waist.

"What are you having, Ruby?" I glance to my side, only

to double take as it seems Wes has planted himself between Ruby and me. He's leaning against the bar top looking suave, and his grin is so incredibly sexy that it's irritating.

"Those were some solid moves on the dancefloor to Salt-n-Peppa," he tells me, and I look quickly behind him to see Ruby is in deep conversation with Wes's friend. This whole situation is transpiring faster than the speed of light.

"It was TLC," I correct him with a little sass. "And what are you doing here?" I must sound slightly unsure of where our conversation is going.

Since I offered myself to him years ago—to which he pushed me away—we haven't seen each other much. Partly due to my college schedule, my spare time once occupied by my boyfriend, now ex. The fact Wes is so busy with work also contributed to that. Life hasn't thrown us together often, and when it has once or twice, we just kept a safe distance from one another. We ignored each other and circled one another like two sharks with a sea of people between us.

This is the first time we've been alone with nobody around. I mean, Ruby is here, but by the stance of her body, I know I've lost her already to the guy Wes was with.

"I'm in town for the weekend to check on my place. Sadie wants to stay there for a while, while she's nannying for the summer," he mentions as he holds a finger up to the bartender who instantly comes to take his order—because clearly Wes has magical powers. "What are you having?" Wes asks.

"Vodka orange. Oh yeah, Sadie mentioned you have an apartment in the city."

When the bartender walks away, Wes's eyes zero in on me with a grin forming on his mouth. "Ah, so you do talk about me."

"No, I do not talk about you. Sadie brought it up," I try to

justify as Wes steps closer to me and his fingertips brush along my bare arm.

"It's good to see you." He speaks into my ear to ensure I can hear, the whole move sending a shudder through my body.

"I guess there are worse things," I reply mundanely.

His mouth hitches up. "You know, you're feistier than I remember."

My eyes roll as the bartender sets some drinks on the top of the bar. Wes quickly slides two drinks to Ruby and his friend who don't even so much as notice.

Grabbing my drink, I quickly take a decent sip to calm my nerves. In truth, I've thought more about Wes than I should.

"How are you?" he loudly whispers into my ear, and his tone tells me he doesn't mean in this moment, he means in general.

A faint lined smile forms on my face. "Good, and you?"

"Can't complain. Guess you couldn't really avoid me in this situation, Chase and Ruby clearly have plans for tonight," he says before taking a sip of his drink, whiskey, I think.

I have to softly grin at that truth. "I haven't been avoiding you, and I think you also get points for averting me."

"We should probably talk about that one day, as I'm not a fan of the avoidance tactic which I don't plan on continuing." Wes closes our distance and rests his hand next to me on the bar, protectively placing his other hand on my side, making everything inside me dance.

"Well, I really don't want to talk about it tonight," I reply simply, my eyes staring at his hand so close to me.

"It's good to see you... not from a distance, I mean."

I almost hear regret in his voice, or maybe I wish for it.

"I hear you're doing well in the hospitality industry. Does

it make you happy?" I wonder, as I never in a million years would have imagined him ending up in that area. I envisioned him in IT startups. Doesn't really matter what he does; apparently he's doing financially well, from what Sadie says.

He laughs. "I do work in hospitality but probably not the image you have in your head. I focus on business development and investing in businesses. I only touch foot in a kitchen once every six months or so."

"What about starting your own business?" I remember all his plans. He wanted something to call his own. Wes had ideas—and good ideas.

That question makes the corners of his mouth tug. "It'll happen. I hear you're doing well in the industry too."

I nod. "So you do talk about me with Sadie," I counter his earlier statement, and it makes the corners of his mouth curve up. It's in that moment that I realize that he's still touching me. I lean into his space, which causes me to breathe out through pursed lips.

"You okay?" He looks at me, amused, yet his voice is tender.

"Yeah, that orange juice must be a little stronger than I thought." My eyes circle the room, anywhere to avoid looking at him.

"Right... it's the orange juice." A grin plays on his lips.

Ruby and Chase interrupt us with the guy placing a hand on Wes's shoulder. "It's a good song. Going to dance," he informs us, and Ruby flashes her eyes at me as she follows him by the hand.

"We're going to dance too." Wes offers his hand to me, and his determination that this is going to happen has an appeal that I don't want to admit.

Reluctantly, yet with all my inhibitions about to snap away and a good dose of alcoholic courage, I take his hand.

The whole journey with him to the dance floor is like foreplay. My mind and body know it, and it feels like it.

Then we dance.

In the middle of the busy dancefloor, like two people who don't have a complicated history. As if it is the most natural thing to do, considering we haven't glanced at one another in months before tonight—it was a Christmas party at his parents' house, I think.

We get lost in the song too.

We step close, then closer, until we move like we both want something.

I'm not shy either. I grind against him as his arms slide around me from behind, and we move to the music, oblivious to anyone around us. I sway my hips with the purpose of looking sexy, and I admit to myself that I'm doing it for him, I'm too curious.

Slowly turning to him, my body taunting him, his long finger hooks under my chin to guide my gaze to him.

"How much have you had to drink?" he asks into my ear, his breath warm.

"Enough to allow me to do this, but I'm still sober enough to know better," I quip, which causes that devilish smirk on his face to come out. My downfall, really.

He locks me in his sight as he keeps an arm around me and sways us ever so slightly, even though the music isn't slow. His thumb on my chin begins to draw a small circle as my eyes hood slowly closed so I can focus on his touch. I feel him moving closer, the heat of his body closing in on me. My lids flick open, and my head moves a few inches into his direction but stops halfway, as if I'm debating what to do.

My head moves again into his path, and before I can decide, his mouth covers my own. Our lips seal together for a soft kiss, and it sets a spark off inside me, both in memories and the feelings I've buried.

But I never could find a shovel good enough to dig myself out of that hole. He's always there in the back of my mind. More than a teenage crush, so much more.

We kiss and continue kissing. Harder. Longer. Waves moving in my head. This is the closest to floating out of water that I have ever felt.

He pulls away and asks me, "Want to get some air?"

I nod yes, which makes him smile, and his knuckles brush my cheek before he interlinks our fingers and walks us out, leading us up the stairs to the rooftop seating area. Outside, the music from the club becomes background noise and the warm late-spring air feels refreshing compared to inside where it was scorching.

There aren't many people, but we find a quiet spot, and in a flash, our mouths fuse together again. His fingers comb through my hair as my head tilts back to allow him to have the best possible position. My body presses into him, and a need ignites in me to feel more of him.

His hands move to run along my body, walking us backward until I'm pressed against the brick wall of the building. The hanging decorative lights illuminate enough that we can see what we're doing, observe one another's facial expression, full of desire.

This is crazy. Possibly stupid.

How is it that we're like two comets who meet and collide as if we were always destined to?

What is this? What are we doing?

I shake it all away. I can enjoy him just for tonight, surely.

"I still want you," he murmurs as he trails kisses down my neck.

"I'm right here," I breathlessly offer. I do want him. I've

always wondered what it would be like with Wes. There must be a reason women flock to him or why he crosses my mind more times than a normal human could count.

He pulls back gently and looks at me, slightly disoriented. He's surprised by my invitation, and as much as it should surprise myself, it doesn't, because I've thought about this in my fantasies and my wishes.

I roll my eyes and grin. "Wes, I think we can establish that what I offered last time is no longer on the menu. I'm not above you fucking me right here," I confirm with what he must already assume, which is that I am no longer the girl waiting for her first time.

He looks at me both surprised and impressed with my candid response. "Christ, don't say things like that to me. You're encouraging me to fuck you right here in the corner."

I give him a sly smile before my arms loop around his neck. "Well, I mean, that's not what I meant... but I'm open to it if y—" He shuts me up with a kiss before breaking for air with our foreheads touching.

"Let me take you to dinner tomorrow?"

I giggle at his question. "I'm hoping breakfast is an option too."

He looks very satisfied with my answer. "That is most certainly an option. But I can also take you to dinner?"

Our noses nuzzle as his hand cups my cheek. "My flight back to the East Coast is tomorrow afternoon."

"I'll take you to the airport," he offers, and I hear the trouble in his tone. Pure mischief.

"Okay... I should probably tell Ruby that I'm about to disappear?" I answer and double-check as I step back to observe him.

He interlaces my hand with his as an answer, and we head back. As he goes to settle the bill, I walk away and look for Ruby. Before I get far, I glance back to Wes who is now nearly hidden behind a blond-haired beauty all too familiar to me.

"Wes!" She smiles widely before throwing her arms around him.

I remember Cassandra. She was Wes's on-and-off girlfriend in high school and maybe college too.

I freeze as Wes looks at me. Cassandra hugs him, awkwardly hanging off of him, and suddenly reality hits me.

What am I doing? Wes and I don't even live in the same city or state or region. He can't even be a one-night stand—he's my best friend's brother, and we're too connected for it to be just one night. Nor do I know his relationship status as of late. He could be on the rebound and I am just that.

This must have all been the alcohol. Oh, wait, maybe it's that brain malfunction that sometimes happens around him.

Swallowing, I make a decision.

I begin to walk away, but Wes steps away from Cassandra and is at my side in a flash. Staring at his hand on me and pain fills me. It could have been our night.

"Emmy, wait, just give me one minute," he pleads.

Giving him a forced tight-lipped smile, I assure him, "It's okay. I need to go and... it's better this way."

MY FOOT TAPS on the gravel at the side of the road as my hands stay firm on my hips.

"Shall we talk about what you think happened?" Wes is firm in tone.

I throw my arms up in the air. "Nothing to talk about."

"Really? Because if I recall correctly, *you* changed your mind about where that night was heading."

I feel kind of pissed off. "Are you kidding me?" My voice raises. "What was I supposed to do? Your ex-girlfriend showed up and it seemed pretty clear that I was just in the way or… I don't know."

Wes rubs his face with his hands, as he seems frustrated. "Do you really think I'm the type of guy to have kissed you if I had been with someone else?"

"Hah!" I point a finger at him. "See? You admit you kissed me. It was you who initiated it."

A smile creeps up on his mouth due to my response. "Answer the question."

"I didn't know what to think. It was all unexpected. I wanted to believe you were a jackass, it made it easier… I know you're not *that* kind of guy."

"Nothing happened between me and her. We stayed in contact as friends, and she wanted to say thank you because I sent her a contact for something."

"It doesn't matter." I try to shake it all off.

"I should have called you. I wish I had," he states simply.

"Wes, it wouldn't have helped our situation. Even if we'd slept together, what good would that have done? We lived in two different places."

He bites his bottom lip. "Now we are very much in the same place," he reminds me, and that thought kept me up last night for an extra hour or two.

I step back immediately, and we stand there in a long pause with the rain drops sprinkling from the clouded sky beginning to fall. "Come on, let's get back in the car," I suggest.

He nods, and we both get back into the car and buckle up.

"Have we cleared the air?" he asks as he puts the fob into the ignition.

"I guess so," I say, knowing we haven't.

He begins to ease back onto the road.

"Good. Check *awkward history recap* off your list," he says matter-of-factly.

"You mean awkward first day on the job with my boss? Yeah, sure. Check that off my list." I'm sarcastic as I fold my arms.

"Now, now, Emmy, boss or not, I am confident that you subtly asked my sister at some point in the last few weeks if I'm bringing a date to her wedding, just as I checked if you are. And since we are both going solo, you'll let me dance with you at the wedding, and then you will ask me if we can get out of there, to which I will reply, 'Great idea, Emmy.'" I hear the humor in his voice, but I know it's mixed with seriousness—and damn him but yes, I *may* have casually asked Sadie if Wes was coming alone. I also asked *before* Wes became my boss.

"No, absolutely not. I want to focus on the events. The last thing I need right now is adding sleeping with my boss— who happens to be you—to the uncertainty of my life." I rest my head against my propped elbow along the window. I'm completely aware that there are no hypotheticals in what I just said; it's 100% true.

"Oh, so you *are* calling me boss, and sleeping with me *did* cross your mind." I don't need to look to know his face is smug.

"I'm serious. From this moment on, we focus on working together. Nothing else," I remind him, since my life plans right now don't include any entanglements with Wes.

"Sure. Whatever you want to think."

I growl. "When did you get so exasperating?" I angle my body to him to watch him as he drives. "It's like this, Wes. Fool me once, shame on me. Fool me twice, shame on you. Twice now in my lifetime I have let my guard down around you, and it never ends well for me." I look away and reposition my body, slightly aggravated that I can't pounce him in this second.

"Not exactly, Emmy. That's where you are wrong." He flashes me a grin, and he almost seems to be rejuvenated.

"Enlighten me, oh wise one, with your knowledge," I say sarcastically.

"Because… third time is always the charm," he tells me almost fondly as we continue on our journey toward wine country hidden amongst corn fields.

The rest of the car ride was a thick silence with only the acoustic covers playing. I considered the drive as a cooling-off period, because by the time we reach the farm, Emily seems to be almost refreshed, as if our trip down memory lane has been brushed under the rug, which is fine by me. As long as I put in my effort to get any awkwardness out of the way, then I don't care how this all transpires.

Okay, not entirely true. I mean, there is only one way I want the next few weeks to unravel, and the ride back may be grueling, as the edging of her dress seems to have made a deal with the devil, the way it rests *just* above mid-thigh when she sits.

Parking the car, we both look at one another. Her mouth slants into a smile as she looks at me. "Ready? This looks beautiful."

Yes, I am genuinely interested in this place, but the idea of a long drive to and from with Emily was my main objective for today.

We both hop out of the car and walk through the stone parking lot with pristine gardens surrounding it. My eyes follow the sway of Emily's hips, and despite the stone path, it's her body that's acting as my trail. The sound of a fountain by the entrance of a refurbished farmhouse is slightly calming as a woman in her mid-fifties comes out the door with an overdone smile.

"You must be the soon-to-be newlyweds," the woman greets us.

That has a nice ring to my ears, but sadly, I'm going to have to correct her.

Emily chortles in response, and I can't help but smile to myself as I scratch my chin. "That is… *not* us. I'm Weston Bay, we spoke on the phone." I offer my hand out to shake.

"Oh, of course you are. I'm Helen. Sorry, you two just have *that* look," she explains before shaking Emily's hand.

We all make a quick round of hellos before Helen suggests a tour and we follow. She explains to us that the farm is owned by three brothers around our age, and she helps out twice a week. The farm-style house is modernized with stone elements and has a small restaurant and bed-and-breakfast. She takes us through to the back patio area where Emily's mouth nearly drops. The view is quite something, the perfect spot for watching a sunset, and I can't help but notice the firepit in the corner. A field fills the horizon, rows of what I would assume are pumpkins and lettuce, all perfectly kept.

"This is amazing, what a backdrop. I bet you have a lot of weddings here." Emily circles around like a kid in a candy store. "I'm guessing bride and groom stand there." She points to a spot at the end of the patio. "Guests here." She points in another direction. "You could easily have hay bales as seating to make it very rustic or little chairs for chic."

"Well, aren't you just precious," Helen pipes in, clearly taken with Emily.

"Sorry, I just see so much potential here. I love farms, and it's so calm out here. Plus, pumpkins and autumn are my favorite time of year."

Is it crazy that I don't care if my business fails, as seeing her like this is worth it?

"Imagine the evenings. We get perfect skies," Helen adds.

"Sounds lovely." Emily smiles.

"How about we quickly finish the tour before the weather turns. Then we can sit inside to try a few things. We just started bottling our own house blend of wine," Helen mentions as her hand indicates to the field.

"Really? Wine, here?" Emily seems surprised.

"Even with our Midwest winters, it's possible. There are more and more wineries popping up in Illinois every year," Helen explains.

"I definitely want to check it out. I'm curious about the timing and when you harvest," I reply and begin to follow the woman.

I can't help but notice Emily in the corner of my eye, looking at me like I said something strange. Then I realize that this must be new for her; she's never seen me while I work.

My thought is confirmed when Emily speaks up with a half-grin. "So, this is Wine-connoisseur Wes. *Huh*, I need to get used to this image."

"Have you two worked together for a long time?" Helen wonders as we walk down the slight hill.

"She's been wanting me to boss her around for years," I answer with innuendo as my hand gently touches Emily's lower back in a natural protective gesture—in case the slope of the yard is too much for her, *obviously*.

Emily is so busy taking in her surroundings that she doesn't notice either my comment or hand. And so goes the next ten minutes of exploring the farm. The pumpkins are too early to be pulled, but inside the farm there are barrels of olive oil and wine. Then we come across livestock, and Emily is in her element again—and it just does something to me.

"They are so cute. Do you make your own cheese here too?" Emily nearly coos as she watches a few cows grazing in the side field, separate to the pumpkins, as we stand in the middle of the gravel between the farm and main house.

"All our produce is grass-fed," Helen explains.

"Organic?" I ask, as I've considered going all organic in the restaurant.

"No, but just as close. It's hard to get organic status with so many big farms nearby, their pesticides are in the air." She sounds a little disgruntled by the fact, and I can understand. It's also why I haven't moved to organic; it's a lot of rules and checks.

"I can imagine," I offer my understanding. "How often do you make deliveries to Chicago?"

"We use a regional delivery service. It usually picks up on Tuesdays and delivers same-day to restaurants we have contracts with, but truthfully, it's only a handful. Excuse me for a second," Helen clarifies before indicating with her finger to wait as she steps away to read something on her cell phone.

Emily adjusts her stance and offers a reassuring smile to me, then in a low tone speaks. "Means they would be unique to your menu, since not many can find Olive Owl's variety of products in the city."

Scratching the back of my neck, I can only agree. "It's appealing, for sure—"

Helen's cheery voice interrupts me as she walks back to us. "By any chance can you two stay for a full tasting?"

"I would definitely like to sample the cheese before

making an order," I answer and notice that Helen's smile seems to say she has other ideas.

"We will make sure that happens, but the couple who are getting married here next month just let me know they have to cancel their taste-testing today, and we already set everything up for them."

"Oh, that's not fun. I can imagine you put in a lot of time to arrange everything," Emily sympathizes.

Helen takes that as our answer and claps her hands together. "Great. You both will stay and do the tasting, so it doesn't go to waste."

Emily looks at me, slightly frozen. A fucking satisfied grin forms on my face, though. Who'd have thought fate would have thrown an intimate meal for two our way today?

Fantastic.

———

HELEN SITS us down at a table in their restaurant near a cold fireplace. A perfect row of glasses and bottles of wine plus a snack plate are waiting for us.

"How about I let you two taste in peace, then we can talk about the items you enjoyed after. We do have a bed-and-breakfast, in case you don't want to make the drive back to Chicago after getting through all of the wine," Helen offers with a bright smile as she uncorks a bottle and sets it on the table. "Just let me know and enjoy." She walks away to leave us be.

While a perfect opportunity has just been presented to us to be stuck with one another for a night, preferably in the same room, I actually plan on being a gentleman. Getting Emily naked and under me is on the agenda, but I set it on the calendar for a few days from now. I know she needs to warm up to me again.

Emily gently shakes her head at me as she sits down. "Don't even ask me. No."

I sit down and quickly defend myself with a charming look. "Hey, staying over is not my idea. I promised your perfect boss is on good behavior today."

She studies me with narrowed eyes, wondering about my motives, I'm sure. But then she turns her attention to the samples on the table and slowly pours our first option of white wine. "I like getting to know Professional Wes. You are really impressing me with your wine knowledge."

"Impressed? Or do I need to tell you this has a nutty smell." I take a sip and let my tastebuds enjoy the wine for a few seconds before swallowing. "It's smooth and dry. Perfect for appetizers, and there is a subtle hint of strawberry as an extra element."

Her eyes go wide with a faint smile forming before she smells her wine and takes a tiny sip. I watch her taste the wine and enjoy the view of her face making funny angles as she does so.

Then… she swallows.

An image that wakes my dick up for a full-on marathon.

I grab a cracker to focus my senses on something else. Emily follows suit and grabs some pepper jack cheese and a cracker.

We both relax onto our seats as we let out a calming exhale. Looking at one another, it feels like we have a fresh page after our conversation earlier.

"Are you happy to be back?" I ask as I lean over to pour our next sample.

"Sure. Why not?" It comes out mundane.

"So, you're not happy to be back? No bullshit, it's me."

She taps the rim of the wine glass. "I don't know what I feel. I got lucky and got a dream job right out of college, had a great apartment, could even travel for work, and then *poof*, it was all gone."

I take a bite of cheese. "You didn't want to stay in Boston?"

She shrugs a shoulder. "Other than the job and apartment, friends were more social acquaintances."

"And no boyfriend."

She looks away then back at me, partially entertained. "I see we are still gathering intel from Sadie on each other, and no… not recently." She sips from her next glass, and I'm surprised she doesn't ask me about my recent romantic history.

"And now you can have the job, the apartment, friends, and the guy who will make you come every night at least three times before the sun comes up." It just rolls out of my mouth, since in all honesty, I can't be that professional around her.

Emily chokes on her wine and sets her glass down abruptly while she clears her throat. "Wes." It's a long, stern tone.

"What? That could be anyone, although I appreciate that your mind just wandered to a place where I am that guy." I give her a teasing look.

She shakes her head but struggles to keep a tugging smile from forming. "I may need to upgrade my sips to full glasses of wine."

"Well, they did offer us a room."

She picks up a cube of cheese, scans the room, then throws it at me. "Boss Wes, please," she reminds me to behave.

"In all seriousness, you're happy you're back?"

She contemplates for a second before answering. "I think so—or hope so. I just need to figure out the career thing, and my apartment is only temporary. I want to make a home somewhere. Truthfully, I feel kind of stuck until everything is figured out. I have a plan, just need to make sure it happens."

Her honesty is endearing, and I decide to turn off my jabs for a second. Instead, I search the spread on the snack plate of appetizers. "If anyone will make their plan work, it's you," I assure her.

"Thanks." Her eyes meet my own and soften. "Why did you come back? Was it because of your dad?"

I pause and realize she always had a tendency to see through me. At times, she understands me more than my own sister. Still, she catches me off guard.

"Yes and no."

"Sadie mentioned once that…"

"What? That I got in an argument with my old man?"

She slowly nods.

"Not exactly. I think he just wanted something else for me, but I went my own way."

"Still? Is it that studying law is not a topic for debate?" She looks at me like it's crazy, and it is, as I am successful, just not from his chosen path.

"But you're both okay together now, right?"

"God, I hope so, otherwise it's going to be a *long* wedding this weekend," I reflect. "I mean, he looked over my contracts. Yet, I feel like he's playing along, waiting for…"

"You to fail?" She looks almost afraid to say that.

"Not afraid to throw the punch, are you?" She's right too. I take a small sip of the wine again. "This one is too fruity for me."

"Me too." She slides her glass to the side. "But he played a factor in your decision to move back?"

"Not fully. I mean, I had decided to open a place a few months ago. Originally, I thought about commuting every few weeks to check on the place. It didn't feel right, though, and after my dad's heart attack then it made sense to be near in case something happened. It helped speed up my decision."

She reaches across the table to touch my hand as a comforting gesture. "I understand. Do you miss Michigan?"

I shake my head slowly, very much aware her hand is still touching my own. "I still go back, as I have a few investments there and it's a good place for business. But, same as you. I had good work, friends who were acquaintances—not like here where long-lasting friendships are. Something was missing."

"Right."

We get a little lost in each other's eyes, as if we've both been missing something in our lives, but maybe not anymore.

"We should probably give ourselves some distance. Alcohol and us don't mix very well. I should probably let go of my boss's hand too," she says, not blinking or leaving my gaze.

"I don't mind. As a matter of fact, your boss may even insist on it." A subtle smile creeps up on my mouth.

I swear she blushes right before she lets my hand go.

"Don't we have food to taste?" Emily reminds me as she looks at the items on the table.

"Apparently the chicken and beef dishes that the bride and groom wanted to try," I say as I stick my fork into a plate of meat.

"Oh, and also the vegetarian pumpkin ravioli too, plus their olive oil and bread."

Without thought, I guide the fork to her mouth. "Try this."

Because our brains don't register much when we're

around each other, her hand brushes along mine to direct the fork to her mouth that envelopes around the silver.

"Mmm, that's good. Wait…did you just feed me?" she realizes, slightly horrified or amused.

I laugh softly in the back of my throat. "You didn't seem to mind."

"Nope." She waves a finger at me and shakes her head side to side. "We are not going down this path. Keep the forks, utensils, and any part of your body on your side of the table."

"Ooh, bossy. Isn't that my role?" I smirk as I grab a sip from my ice water.

She throws her napkin to the table in frustration. "Right, work. It's why we're here and not your ploy to get me alone in the middle of nowhere." She raises a brow at me with a smirk.

"Emmy, trust me, we didn't need to leave the city for me to get you alone. Shall we focus on the selection?"

"You're optimistic, but sure, boss, lets focus on the food."

An hour later we resorted to small sips of wine, water, and a lot of snacking and sampling of food. When Helen returns, we tell her our take on the food and wine, all favorably good. Then I confirm an order.

She claps her hands together. "Are you sure you don't want to stay over? It's going to start storming in about thirty minutes according to the forecast. They've issued a tornado watch too."

Geez, Mother Nature is really conspiring with my dick today.

I look at my watch and see it's only 4pm. We could easily still drive back and, even with traffic, still return at a decent time. I don't debate it. "I think we'll manage, but now we have a reason to come back."

Helen arrives with a small gift bag and hands it to Emily.

"I *love* the cloth tote bag and the design." Emily beams as she looks over the bag with an owl on it.

"A little sneak peek at some other products. Some samples of pumpkin butter, honey-scented candles, and brochures for when we have our upcoming couples' retreat weekends." Helen squinches her nose in excitement.

"Oh?" Emily is amused enough.

"Well, I just thought you two would want to come back to try our romantic package." She winks at Emily.

Emily begins, "That's, uhm, thoughtful but—"

Without hesitation, I interrupt. "So sweet of you, we will definitely consider and let you know when we book a reservation."

Emily gives me a death stare that only I would know, while her professional smile doesn't fade.

We all say our goodbyes, and despite the heavy rain, we run to the car. The moment we close the doors and wipe droplets of water off our faces, we turn to one another.

"You had to throw in that last comment, didn't you?" She gives me knowing eyes.

"You loved it."

"Just drive, Wes. I want to get home; I have a lot to do tomorrow."

I look outside the windshield at the pouring rain. "I'm sure you do. I know I hired someone who meticulously plans."

"True." She leans back and gets comfortable as hail begins to hit the glass. "That's not reassuring," Emily says as she looks out the window.

"Maybe we wait a few minutes before heading off?"

"Probably a good idea."

A calming silence takes over as the hail and rain pours.

Side-glancing to Emily and our eyes lock. Her hair is slightly out of place and damp. So fucking sexy too.

"This is an odd first day on the job."

"But you enjoyed every second."

She snorts. "That's a stretch."

I can't help it and I have no regrets in what I am about to do.

"Oh, so if I touch you like this then your body has no reaction?" I say as I reach to tuck her loose strand of hair behind her ear before my fingertips trace the outline of her jaw and her head moves back. Her breath catches, and I can see her chest heaving up and down.

"Nope. No reaction." She's a little defiant today.

I move closer to her, my head tilting so my lips can tease the corner of her mouth. The air between us evaporates, and to be honest, my own heart races slightly, especially when my lips are so close to her skin yet do not melt onto her.

"Don't you dare, Weston Bay," she whispers a plea but doesn't move, and instead her hand grips my wrist and holds me in place so I cannot pull away.

Brushing my mouth along her cheek, I whisper, "What? Kiss you? Is that what you want me to do?"

"Wes—"

I move to barely touch her lips as I inhale her delicious, sweet scent. She even moves to tease me, to encourage me. *Oh*, she wants my lips on hers.

The sound of thunder startles her, and in that instant, she retreats back slightly, causing space to return between us.

Internally, I groan that I was so close as I return to my side of the car.

"Sounds far away." Okay, she's using the avoidance tactic again. She glances at her hands on her lap before looking back at me. "You're familiar." Her soft tone grabs my attention. "Even if time passes, we're always the same around one another." She studies me for a second to ensure I'm grasping her words, and I will listen to her for eternity. "Promise me we will focus. You and I both need your opening to be a success." Her look is pleading, as if it pains for her to say it.

Emily reminds me of one truth, but the fact she isn't enjoying her request shows that I am one step closer with her, and today, that's victory enough.

EMILY

Blowing out a breath, I stare at my wall of post-it notes as I stand in my towel with a fruit smoothie in hand. It's a rainbow of colored paper carefully organized by sections of my life. Pink for career path, yellow for current work, blue for apartment, and orange for hobbies.

There is no room on my board for romance, dating, or anything that constitutes as complicated predicaments with Wes. It's both frustrating and wise. I need to focus on work. Already the research into going freelance has given me a headache. Between figuring out health insurance and starting an LLC, I need to keep my head strong and clear.

But why, oh why, did Wes have to stroll back into my life now? Seeing him in the flesh causes an ache of want for the man, but I can't get distracted.

Wes has always been one of those guys who naturally has smooth moves with no effort on his part. He was born to drive the female population wild. He was always sweet with me, but this time around he seems… persistent, determined, and like he has delicious plans for me. It's so fucking hot too.

Yesterday in his car I wanted his lips on mine. I wanted to

kiss him so hard that we wouldn't even care if a tornado was nearby. We would create our own.

But sense knocked into me, and after the rain settled, the car ride back was quiet except for the occasional talk about Sadie and Logan. Even when Wes dropped me off and his eyes blazed with the same curiosity as my own, we kept it… simple.

Simple is what I need right now.

I shake my head at my wall to snap me back into action mode. I decide to get dressed. A teal dress to mid-thigh, ankle boots, and my notebook in hand.

When I arrive at the restaurant, Charlie greets me with his usual smile. "Morning."

"Morning," I reply and then notice he's throwing very wet towels into the sink. "Everything okay?"

"Yeah, just had one of the beer taps leak. Not the best way to start the morning, but an easy fix. You? A lot on the agenda for today?"

I lean over the bar top to get a glimpse of the mess on the floor. "A lot, actually. Want to look into some goody bag options for the invitees for the opening? Do you have ten minutes?"

Charlie looks up at me and tries to suppress his grin. "It's best you talk with Wes. He just got the branding back from the designer, and truthfully, I need to focus on ensuring the new valets are up to speed."

I offer him a reassuring look. "It's okay, I'll go find him now. Wes is in his office?" I point upstairs, and Charlie nods.

Heading up to Wes's office, I admire how the restaurant already looks ten times better than a few days ago. Every day it seems like it's more ready for the whole world to see.

Arriving at Wes's office, I knock on the frame of the open door.

"Just wanted to... oh, I..." I struggle for words as my mouth gapes open at the sight in front of me. #Thirstythursday just jumped off my social media feed into real life.

Wes is half-dressed, searching for what I hope to the man upstairs is a shirt in his gym bag. His body is more toned and muscled than the last time I saw him this way, and that is a damn hard task to do.

Ahhh.

"Want to watch me undress? I mean, if you insist." His haughty look tells me he enjoys the fact that my eyes can't seem to look away.

I walk slowly into the room and swallow. "Beer tap get to you too?"

"Yep, and luckily, I had a spare clean shirt in my gym bag."

I bite my inner cheek. "I can see the gym is a frequent destination for you."

He laughs at my remark and his eyes go wide. "Any surprises I should know about?"

"For when?" I look at him, confused.

"For when I see you naked."

"Wishful thinking." I should be annoyed with his persistence, but I would be a fool not to enjoy the fact that I make this man act this way.

"I guess it's been a while. You never got to see the goods during our against-the-wall tryst." He says it as straight-faced as possible.

I move past his quip. "Yep. A while. So, I am going to stop staring at you now. Highly inappropriate—" *Crap, I'm scolding myself aloud.*

"Your boss disagrees." The man actually winks at me. He must get his kicks out of this situation.

I shake my head slowly as my tongue circles my teeth while he scrunches his shirt then pulls it on. "I want to arrange party favors for the opening but don't have an idea on colors. Plus, we should go over the schedule again."

"Come here." He indicates for me to sit next to him behind his desk.

I don't think much about it until I am actually sitting next to him with our arms grazing and that familiar anticipation running through me. His masculine scent with a touch of spice hits my nose, and I hope it rubs off onto me, because I like to torture myself that way.

"Okay, so we have the opening in a few weeks, my dad's event next weekend, and a staff dinner next Wednesday. I also want to get in two business lunches for the marketing firm we're using and probably one of Logan's clients," he lists as he shows me the calendar on his screen.

"That's not a problem. I'll make a few table settings to see which style you want for the opening and your dad's event. Any particular colors that pique your interest?"

He spins in his desk chair so he's facing me, and it causes our knees to graze, sending a fucking earthquake to between my legs. What's even more unfair is the fact that it would be so easy to wrap my arms around his neck right now, as if he were mine.

Wes leans forward with purpose then his arm crosses between us as our eyes hold. His finger loudly jabs a button on the keyboard of his laptop. He must know what he does to me. I glance at the screen to a beautiful logo of black, dark blue, and gold.

The name still gets to me. I'm almost in awe that he remembers what I once told him while lying in his arms or that it would even cross his mind still.

…But I am not sure he needs to gain any points. He's already high on my list. Just, now isn't the time for us.

I clear my throat and decide to speed past it all. "I will keep it in mind when I choose colors and themes. It's a beautiful logo."

"Yeah, Layla did well. Do you know her? Josh is the owner of one of the marketing companies I utilize—his wife, Layla, did all of this." He clicks away his screen to sleep mode.

"I met her a few times, since she sometimes hangs with Sadie. She's really sweet. Shall I contact her to make a few place cards for the opening dinner?" I open my notebook, ready to take notes.

"For sure. You should talk to her about your own plans too. She freelances if you need advice on that."

I look up with a smirk. "Already trying to get rid of me?"

Wes leans back in his chair and crosses his arms. "No, the opposite, actually, but if you want to go learn more about freelancing, then you should give her a call. Plus, I'll support you in whatever you decide to pursue. Unless you want to go back to corporate events?"

Quickly I shake my head no. "Nah, I much prefer smaller events. At the farm yesterday I was truly jealous of whoever gets to plan the weddings there, and here, it's small dinner and lunch functions. People have fun at those, they're always celebrations, not an event to sell something."

"So you like when people have something to celebrate?"

My head tilts side to side as I think about it. "Exactly. Anyhow, I should get busy on my to-do list today," I mention as I tap my notebook with my pen.

Wes abruptly stands up and holds his hand out to me. "Come on, let me show you something first."

"I hope it's not the cellar downstairs, as that place freaks me out," I say as I take his hand, and he pulls me up to join him.

"Don't go down there. Send one of the guys if you need something. But no, escaping to dark corners and having my way with you will have to be for another time." He's sarcastic, but only 75% if I know him well enough.

He lets my hand go when we walk out of his office, and I follow him. We stop at the end of the small hall, and he searches for the keys in his pocket then pulls them out to unlock a door that I assumed was a closet. It appears to be a small flight of stairs, and he tilts his head in the direction of the stairwell.

I smile curiously and follow him, holding my notebook. The moment we reach the top, the bright blue morning sky hits me. The rooftop area is nothing special, but the views are spectacular. A clear view over the Chicago River, and the buildings surrounding the water are spread before us. If you look into the distance, you can see where the lake meets the mouth of the river.

"Wow, this is gorgeous. I had no idea you could get up here." I cautiously approach the ledge.

"I love it, but sadly we'll never be able to get a permit to make it part of the restaurant—well, for guests anyway," he explains as he touches my elbow for extra safety. "Careful."

I don't move farther, but I turn my attention to Wes. "I feel like I'm not even in the middle of the city. It's peaceful up here."

"I think so too. Nothing like the farm yesterday, but it's halfway close, and I like that."

His thought makes my lips part. "Ah, so you aren't a city boy at heart."

The deep laugh from him sounds so smooth and natural. "I wonder what image you have of me sometimes."

I shrug my shoulders and look at my foot playing with a few pebbles. "I sometimes wonder too." Some days I imagine him with a model on his arm in a busy club, and other times I know he was once happy with sounds of nature and the night sky.

We both go quiet as we look around at the panoramic view.

"This is really something. You know how to pick good real estate; your apartment is also amazing," I say as I recall his industrial-feeling penthouse.

"How do you know what my place looks like?" he wonders and touches my arm to ensure I answer him, with our eyes on each other.

My tongue runs along my lip then licks the corner of my mouth. "Oh yeah, during our trip down memory lane yesterday I forgot to mention that I slept in your bed once."

"Uhm, pretty sure I would remember that," he doubts me. "Confident it would have been an out-of-this-world, stop-the-clock kind of night too."

"Oh, would it?" I give him knowing eyes. "Last summer, after a night of drinking, Sadie and I found ourselves wandering back to your bachelor pad where she was staying, so I stayed rather than head back to my parents. You would've been privy to this, but you don't spend much time there. Your bed is pretty comfortable." I wiggle my eyebrows to tease him.

Wes rakes a hand through his hair. "This is news. Happy my bed could be of service, and even more relieved you ended up in my bed and not someone else's."

"I'm not that kind of person, you caught me on an off night," I tell him because I think he's insinuating that one night in the club.

He steps closer to me and his fingertips land on my hips. "You know we also went to a rooftop briefly a year ago too."

My eyes side-roll as I bite my bottom lip, and I debate what to say. "Well… I should get back to work. I think I'll head to a few florists to get some samples and check out quality with price."

Yet, I don't step back, nor does he.

"Sure."

"Charlie gave me the full invite list, and I was looking over it. There are a few highlighted names. Do you need me to contact—"

"No! It's uh… it's okay." He scratches the back of his neck and looks extremely uncomfortable.

I place a hand on my hip and study him. "Something I should know?"

He shakes his head no.

"Would you tell me if there was?" I doubt.

Wes reaches his hand out to touch my shoulder. "Relax. I'll leave all the planning stuff to you, and we can go over it when you need to."

"Sure." I still wonder if there's a mystery I should be uncovering.

We begin to walk toward the stairs down but stop when I touch his arm. "Really, Wes, this place is going to be amazing, with or without the rooftop. The menu already looks so delicious, and the dining area has a perfect view. I feel like I'm walking around a magazine."

"Emmy." His knuckle slides along my cheek. "You always have so much confidence in me, and I appreciate it. But for the last thirty seconds I barely heard you because I can't get something off my mind, especially with that news that you've been in my bed…" He gives me that charming grin that is impossible to say no to. "Just tell me that you'll save some time and a dance for me at the wedding."

I squint my eyes and I survey him for his motives—it's all I ever seem to be doing these last days.

"Maybe."

"I can work with maybe." He's satisfied and begins to walk away.

"By the way," I call out, and he stops and turns to me, curious. "I have a tattoo." I let it sink in, and he looks perplexed. "You asked about any surprises of the body variety earlier. It's something you definitely did not get to see before." I flash my eyes at him, and I'm completely aware I'm toying with him.

He seems to enjoy this new fact. "Oh?" His voice raises in surprise as he scrubs a hand across his jaw. "What and where? This is vital information that must be shared. My brain is already imagining a few possibilities on your body."

A very sultry smile spreads across my face. "Somewhere not appropriate for my boss to see, and what it is? A mystery you want to find out." I wink before walking in front of him down the stairs, knowing full well he is eyeing my sway that I… okay, I add a little extra movement to.

At some point today, I've decided I approve of harmless flirting.

WES

"This is a good steak tartare," Logan notes as he sets his fork to the side. My future brother-in-law wears a suit and a perpetual grin on his face. As much as the guy is sometimes cocky, he is a perfect gentleman to my sister, and I can see he loves her.

"The tuna steak was cooked to perfection too," Cole adds, tugging at his equally expensive suit. Although he is Logan's best friend, lately we've gotten close, as two bachelors living in the city.

We're sitting in my restaurant eating lunch. Although not open yet, I need feedback on the menu options.

"You're going to be okay sitting with your folks on Saturday?" Logan asks as he takes a drink from his club soda.

I scratch my chin. "Sure."

"Convincing enough." Logan laughs. "And I take it having Ems at the table won't be an issue either?" He indicates his head to the other side of the restaurant toward a separate reception room.

For the last two hours, she has been whizzing around the

place creating sample bouquets and working with Charlie on table settings.

"Why would it be?"

Cole looks at me, impressed. "Is there history there? Did I miss the memo?"

"What do you mean memo?" I'm slightly defensive.

"Well, I was going to ask her to dance since she is the maid of honor and I'm the best man. But if that's crossing a line then tell me now or forever hold your peace," Cole explains casually, and the guy, although decent, is the type who would charm his way into a date or two.

"She will be occupied so don't concern yourself with dancing-partner services," I inform him in a sharp tone.

Cole looks at Logan who shrugs. "Don't look at me. Sadie only says those two have a weird relationship and she's also clueless."

My eyes wander to Emily who walks to the bar to collect some scissors before walking back toward the corner of the room. Her skirt today was made for the sole purpose of torturing me for hours.

"This place is going to be great. I sent you some people to add to the guest list," Logan mentions. Since Logan and Cole are big names in the business world, I don't mind them putting their VIP clients on the list.

"Cool, and I'm using Ives & Wells for marketing."

"Oh good, be sure to give Noah hell," Cole jokes, but he's probably serious, as Noah Wells is dating his sister and his sister now works for Logan. We are all basically interconnected.

"I'll do my best," I reply.

"Hey, did you end up selling your real estate in Detroit?" Cole asks as he circles the ice cubes in his glass.

"No, I kept it all. A good investment, a reserve in case this place doesn't work," I explain.

"This place will work, for sure. Good location, good menu, and a woman to drive you crazy," Cole assures me with a grin.

"Something tells me the woman factor isn't as easy as I thought. She's taking a little extra work," I admit, but I'm still not deterred.

"Why? The boss/employee scenario works wonders," Logan reminds us all.

I shake my head at him. "Again. Not having that conversation with you, considering how you met my sister." I frown and cluck the inside of my cheek. My sister was the nanny when he had guardianship of his nephew, and Logan was her boss. It made me scratch my head a few times when she told me.

Logan sighs with a smile. "Fuck. I'm going to be married this weekend."

"I hope that's a good thing, otherwise this lunch is going to get awkward really quick." I look at him, amused, to which he replies with a warm smile.

"It is," he assures me.

"Now you need to be next so we can have another bachelor party." Cole gives me raised brows. He had planned Logan's bachelor party which was a poker night with a stripper that my future brother-in-law had no interest in. Cole, on the other hand, had no problem filling in on the role.

"Well, I need to head back to the office to finish up a bunch of work before I'm off for a while," Logan says as he stands and buttons his suit jacket.

"I'll head too. Wes needs to put the moves on the woman who keeps catching his eye," Cole adds as he also stands.

"Yeah, yeah, yeah. Anyhow, thanks for stopping by."

I walk them out, talk a few logistics in terms of the wedding this weekend, then say goodbye. As I head over to the bar, Emily looks up from creating some odd napkin creature.

She gives me a gentle smile. "Everything good in groom land?"

"Yeah, he's ready to make my sister an honest woman," I joke.

Emily swats my arm in response.

"Where's Charlie?" I ask.

"Calling a supplier or something."

"Nice. One less thing on my list to do."

"You need to check if you like the table layout." She waves me to follow her.

This place is big enough. On a good night, I hope to have all hundred seats filled. We arrive to the separate room that we will use for private parties and can fit another forty people. Immediately, my head retreats back, as it looks completely different.

"Oh." She sounds disappointed. "You don't like it?"

My mouth quickly forms a smile. "The opposite, actually. I love it. I'm just surprised at how different it looks."

The table has a white tablecloth with white dishes combined with centerpieces of crimson and white flowers and candles in industrial-type lanterns. It's not feminine, but just the right amount of classy.

Relief floods her face, and suddenly she looks proud of herself as her lips quirk out.

"Really, it looks great."

"You only want one or two flowers on the table, otherwise it gets overwhelming. Everyone loves candles so that's a must, and then for the opening, you should do a really long table for the dinner…" She goes on and on about candles, name cards, and many things, but I don't understand a word, as I'm too mesmerized by her energy and beauty.

I look at her and I feel relaxed, like this new business venture may just be a success. Her eyes twinkle and her smile doesn't fade. She tries to avoid my gaze, otherwise I know that shade of pink will appear on her face.

"Any other questions, boss?" She clears her throat, and her hand straightens her skirt.

"No… I guess I will see you for the big day."

Our eyes meet and I'm beginning to wonder if I screwed myself out of another possible scenario. The one where she doesn't have the boss rule, where we would have met for the first time in a while at the wedding and then reconnected before ripping each other's clothes off. Would I have had more of a chance if I weren't her boss?

———

SADIE, to my surprise, opted for a simple and small wedding. She also decided to skip the whole rehearsal dinner and kept it to one place for the wedding and reception. Not that it deters the media from trying to get the intel on the successful Logan Jax marrying at last.

As much as I would have loved for her to have her wedding at Jupiter, it makes sense they have it at the Grand Club—the place where they met.

It's one of those old dinner clubs, and although stuffy for my tastes, it has a great view and menu, so I can't fault her choice.

I also can't complain that I got off scot-free on the brother-of-the-bride responsibility train. A small wedding means I can sit in the crowd and don't have to worry about any groomsman shit.

Staring at Sadie and even I may feel a tear forming somewhere. My little sister looks beautiful, elegant, and happy. I hand her the flowers as we stand in her room where my mother is busy in the corner straightening her hair.

"Looking good, Sis," I tell her, and she smiles at me. "The groom arrived so that's a good sign," I tease her, and she softly hits me.

"Big brother to the very end, huh?"

"Absolutely. But seriously, it's going to be a perfect night. Now, do you need me to do anything?"

"No, I think Emily is out there somewhere checking things, even though it's not her role."

Just the mention of her name and I get excited. I haven't seen her yet. "Yeah? Where is she, do I need to go find her?"

My sister looks at me, slightly perplexed. "Being her boss is really putting you both in a good mood… I asked her to check on Cole since he has best-man duties." Sadie has a straight face, but I feel like she's testing me.

"Oh?" I squeak out.

Sadie smiles. "Or maybe I've been pushing that to see which one of you would slip and prove my theory." She gives me a pointed look. "Obvious," she mumbles as she looks again in the mirror.

"That's my cue to give you some space and grab a drink at the bar." I hug her quickly and whisper in her ear, "Have a long and happy life with Logan. You two were meant to be."

I begin to walk away, and she touches my arm. "Clue me in when fate steps in for you two." She winks at me before returning to her view in the mirror, and I have to smile to myself.

A few minutes later, I'm standing at the bar and taking a sip of my scotch as I scan the arriving guests. It's almost time for the late-afternoon vows. The clearing of a deep voice tells me that when I turn to my side that my father will be staring at me with his perpetual I-know-better smirk to accompany his peppered dark gray hair.

"A scotch on the rocks for me," he requests from the barman.

I look at my father with a raised brow. "Positive that shouldn't be on your menu, considering your health."

He slaps my back with a subtle knowing smile. "Something tells me you don't particularly care."

I scrub a hand across my jaw and now I have to smile to myself. "Really? You want to get into this at my sister's wedding?"

"Tell me, how is your hobby going?"

I bite my inner cheek to stop from speaking my mind. I'm aware this is my sister's big day, after all. Scanning the room once more, I step closer to my father and lower my voice. "It's not a hobby, as you would know when you looked over the contracts and learned that my bank account may just have a higher balance than yours," I refute with slight aggression.

"Right, and why is that?" he asks as he nods a thanks to the barman for handing him his glass.

I laugh bitterly under my breath. "You really want to believe the worst in me, which is oddly funny considering what you and Mom have gotten up to recently."

My father invades my space, also eyeing the room. "Weston, this isn't the time or place. Perfect family today for Sadie," he reminds me of the image we need to maintain.

I take another sip of my drink and smooth my tie. "For Sadie, no problem, but only for Sadie," I remind him.

"Exactly. Follow my lead tonight, okay?"

My blood boils. "Absolutely not."

"Weston," my father warns me in a harsh, low tone.

I'm about to respond, but I follow my father's eyesight to our side.

"Oh, there you are, Mr. Bay. Sadie is ready for you now." Emily offers him a smile that I know all too well is exaggerated, but he assumes is purely genuine.

He offers Emily a half-smile. "Thank you, Emily. It's so good to have you here for Sadie. Her day wouldn't be complete without you." My father nods before walking off.

I turn my attention to Emily, and I feel like the wind has just been knocked out of me. Emily stands there with her hair partly up, wearing a dark purple satin dress that could very well be painted onto her every curve. All we need is the thermostat down a degree or two and I am sure I would see something I very much like. Christ, did my sister pick this dress out? That's what brides do, right? I mean, Emmy is going to steal the fucking show. My head moves to look slightly behind her and notice that there is a lack of fabric.

Fuck me, we're doomed.

"Emmy." I'm a man completely mesmerized.

She nibbles her bottom lip and gives me a confident knowing look, sending my thoughts into a fantasy of her doing that as she lies under me.

"You look… well, you… you look beautiful. Something I would prefer to keep just for my eyes, but we can talk about that after toasts," I tell her as I scratch my cheek, trying to keep my body in check.

Our eyes catch and she smiles gently. "Thanks. This side of you isn't so bad either."

"This night sounds promising then." We can't stop staring at one another, and it dawns on me that she interrupted my father and me. "My dad didn't need to go to Sadie, did he?"

She gently shakes her head. Her protective streak is kind of adorable.

"Your mom seems to have everything under control back in Sadie's dressing room. We'll start in a few minutes."

I step closer to her and touch her hands hanging by her sides. Closing the distance between us, I scan the room then lean in to speak next to her ear. "Thanks, but next time you interrupt me it better be for that dance."

● 9

EMILY

"My money is on one of Logan's baby nieces having a meltdown," Cole tells me as he sits back down at our dinner table after having just given a best-man speech that, although hilarious, was borderline roasting Logan. He's the best man, I'm the maid of honor, and only one of us seems to be taking our roles seriously.

My speech was pretty tame. The usual program of a few memories from when we were teenagers talking about our future selves and how happy Sadie was when she phoned me after she had just met Logan and it was clear he was the one. Then I finished the toast with a cheesy quote about the sky going empty since a star falls every time Logan and Sadie think of one another, which earned me a respectable *aww* from the guests.

I pinch Cole's arm. "Can you please channel positive energy on your best friend's wedding day?"

I'm busy looking around to ensure the venue's event planner didn't screw up any details. I purposely arrived early to check that the cupcake cake was put together to perfection and that the tables were set with elegance for this evening wedding.

"Relax, Ems, they already nailed down the vows, and everyone enjoyed the $400-per-plate dinner," Cole reminds me before he excuses himself.

As soon as he's gone, his vacant chair is filled with Ruby plopping herself on the seat. She was there when Sadie met her husband so of course she's here.

"So, what's the deal with you and Wes?" she asks as she takes a decent sip of red wine while she indicates her head to where Wes is sitting across the table speaking to Logan's sister.

"What do you mean?"

Ruby laughs. "Come on. Every girl in high school crushed on Wes, and you would have to be blind not to see he's looking mighty fine as Adult Wes in that charcoal suit. Plus, I was a witness to you and him getting mighty close that one time—"

"Nothing happened," I remind her.

Ruby gives me a skeptical look. "You two have been eyeing one another for the past two hours. Not to mention, you both pretty much blew up those group photos with your glances, we all noticed."

I adjust my neck at the discomfort of hearing those words from Ruby, as she's a wild one, and the way she's looking across the table has me on full alert that she is preying on her next meal.

"He's my boss," I attempt to divert by stating the obvious.

Ruby looks at me with a mischievous grin. "We are literally at a wedding for Sadie who fucked her boss, and now they're married. But fine, I'll go ask Wes to dance since you don't seem to mind." She begins to stand.

Quickly I grab her arm and drag her back to sitting, which causes her grin to grow.

"*Fine*. You may have a point. Is it warm in here? I really should speak to someone about the air conditioning. Yeah, definitely going to check on that," I ramble as I grab my wine glass and leave the table.

Looking around the room as I walk away and I notice Sadie stealing a kiss with her now husband, and I can't help feeling slightly somber. I'm happy for her, I really am. It's just… wow, she's lucky. Her life ended up with every duck in a row, from her job to finding the one. I don't think I even have one duck in a row, despite my meticulous planning. Instead, I'm floating among uncertainty of what is going to happen on all fronts of my life.

Heading outside, the gentle evening breeze hits me as soon as I step out onto the balcony, surrounded by white fairy lights. Leaning against the railing, I let out a deep breath.

"Penny for your thoughts?" Wes asks as he comes to stand by my side and also looks out across the world below.

"Nothing. Just a perfect day for Sadie. She looks beautiful in her dress, and Logan nearly teared up at the vows. Hell, I think even you nearly shed a tear. Everything was perfect…"

His arm nudges my own. "Something on your mind?"

I glance to my side and see he isn't looking at the world below, he's looking at me.

"I'm happy for her."

"It's just…?" He encourages me to continue.

"She's lucky, that's all. Her life plan is exactly what she wanted, and she got it all before she's twenty-five. My life feels so average in comparison. I haven't had anything in my life yet that feels exceptional."

"Is that a little jealousy I hear?"

I softly gasp as his suggestion. "I'm not… well… maybe."

He turns around so his back leans against the ledge. "It's okay. I feel a little jealous too. They are so perfect together it's hard to stomach some days, and it seems like Sadie and Logan just have it all together."

I reflect on what Wes says. "You're not exactly struggling either, Wes. I mean, you're about to launch a successful business."

He smiles subtly as his hands find his pockets. "There are a lot of risks with it, Emmy. Slightly nerve-wracking too, as I haven't dived into business in Chicago yet."

I guess we are more alike than I realized. Except his level of starting a business is about ten levels higher than mine.

Shivering slightly from the breeze, I decide to change our topic. "How are you doing? Staying clear of your parents?"

"Yeah, I am, but it doesn't bother me enough." He begins to take his suit jacket off.

"What happened?" I ask as he brings his jacket behind me then drapes it over my shoulders. I give him an appreciative look, as it is a little nippy out.

Wes looks away then back at me, debating what to say. "He doesn't like how I ended up with my money."

I give him a puzzled look. "Which is?"

A proud look sweeps across his face. "I won big in a *legal* poker tournament. That helped me invest in some property in Michigan, plus I was paid well for my actual job."

My mouth opens in complete shock. "Really? Poker?"

He nods yes.

"I would… never have guessed. Wow. Wait… is that how you know Charlie?".

"I did meet Charlie at a poker match. He doesn't do it

anymore. Me neither. It was a one-time thing, but the disapproval from the old man is everlasting."

"That's why things seemed a little tense between you and your dad?" I'm still curious, as I get the feeling that there's more.

"One of the things, but I don't want to talk about it tonight. I'm waiting for *another* question." His eyes pierce me, and the tilt of his mouth is pure smolder.

"What would that be?" I tip my head to the side.

The feeling of his fingers gently brushing a few loose strands of my hair behind my ear sends an electrifying chill down my spine.

"You know what I'm waiting for."

My heart feels like it may jump out of my chest and suddenly I feel warm again.

"What? If you like the fairy lights and maybe we should use something similar for your opening?" I'm serious and trying to avoid what he wants to hear and what I want to say.

It makes him grin as he steps a little closer to me.

"We are off the clock. No work."

I swallow, lick my lips, and quickly glance around to see that we're all alone, as everyone's dancing inside.

Looking back at Wes and in my head I recall a few of the scenarios that have run rampant in my head the last few weeks, knowing very well we would both be here tonight.

I'm not tipsy from the champagne or wine, but I do feel like my world is about to spin. It's Weston Bay. He has a tendency to make me feel that way.

"Dance with me. Right here, Emmy," he demands as his arm encircles my waist to pull me close.

"Okay." My answer is feathery and light.

Our bodies meet in the middle, and we begin to slowly sway as I splay my hands against his hard chest. The sound of a slow song in the background might as well be off, as I'm too enthralled by the man touching me to notice anything else.

"I'm on to you, Weston."

"Why, whatever do you mean?" He pulls us closer together then clasps my hand against his chest and spins me gently around and a little sound of surprise escapes me.

"Offering me your jacket, dancing with me under the stars… wasn't this all part of your play?" The look on my face isn't of a woman annoyed or angry—I'm the total opposite.

"There isn't an elaborate ploy. However, this seems like a good start to get us to our destination." He grins that look he flashed my way when I was eighteen and kissing him on the bench swing, the look he has thrown in my direction a few times this week.

"What destination is that again?" My eyes blink as my cheekbones raise from the amusement of his polished moves that are not exactly unaffecting.

When he brushes his lips against my forehead, I'm positive I am about to melt into a puddle. The gruff feeling of his perfect stubble against my skin, combined with his firm soft lips, is pure poison.

"The one where you say let's get out of here and I tell you great idea, because I know it's crossed your mind more than once."

He is completely right, but I need to think smart.

"It's not a great idea," I attempt to caution us and tremble all at the same time.

"It's a perfect idea." He kisses my forehead, and I remember the days when I would lie in his arms and he would pepper kisses all around my face.

Wes was so sweet, patient, and warm with me… until he

broke my heart like many teenage hearts in our zip code, without thought. But looking in his eyes now and I see something different. More grit, more persistence, and something else that I can't pinpoint it, but I still trust it."

"Wes, maybe—"

"Hey, you—Oh, nice, you two. Sorry to *clearly* interrupt," Cole calls out to us from the doorway.

Wes and I immediately look to Cole who seems to enjoy that he's caught us in a perfectly innocent moment filled with dirty thoughts.

"You're both wanted inside for the next round of festivities. Something about throwing flowers and whiskeys for the guys before the happy couple heads out to their action-packed wedding night," Cole quickly explains before heading back in as he drinks from his glass.

Stepping away from Wes, I swing the jacket off my shoulders and give it back. "We should go."

He grips my arm gently. "We *should* go, after whatever the hell the happy couple has planned."

I don't answer and instead beeline it inside to where everyone is gathering, never glancing back at Wes, as it scares me that I may combust.

Arriving inside, Sadie immediately smiles at me and indicates for me to join in by waving her red-and-white bouquet.

"Good. Someone found you." She looks curiously behind me to the far-off distance then back to me. "Funny, my brother just came from the same direction. Something you want to…" Sadie wiggles her eyebrows at me.

I shake my head no. "Nothing to tell you."

"Oh." I could swear she sounds disappointed. "You know, if there were—"

My hands gently shake her cap-sleeved shoulders. "Hey, bride, let's focus on you. What do you need?"

Her beaming smile grows larger if that is humanly possible. "Just wanted to say thank you. I know you chased the event planner, double called the bakery for the cupcakes even though it wasn't your job, and you have just been the best today. Oh yeah, thank you for not roasting me during toasts."

"It's your wedding day. It'll happen only once—unless you're a Kardashian. You have been talking about this day since I met you and you thought you would marry the hot dad from *Twilight*, which explains your taste in slightly older men," I remind her then pull her into a hug.

"He isn't that much older than me, and exactly, I will marry only once, so you will stand in prime location to catch the bouquet and be the next one to marry." She isn't going to budge.

Pulling back, I give her the stink-eye. "Are you rigging the bouquet throwing? Because that's slightly unethical and Ruby may kill you," I tease her.

"I'll take my chances since I think you're a lot closer to finding the one." Sadie winks at me before pushing me in the direction of the dancefloor.

A little later, with a bouquet of flowers from the bride in my hand and with the happy couple heading off to their wedding night, I grab my purse and look around. A wave of disappointment hits me when I don't see Wes. It's probably for the best, as I need to work with him the next few weeks, and tonight I'm feeling a stir of emotions and want.

I make my way to the hallway and elevators, smiling to myself as I look at the flowers. I kind of like the idea of what the tradition means, a twinge of unexpected hope sparking in me.

As I press the button on the wall, my pointed finger is met by a hand that I am all too familiar with.

Peering up to my side, I see Wes looking quite confident,

and I notice the loose buttons at the collar of his shirt, as he took his tie off.

"There is no way we are ending our night." His tone is pure seduction and his eyes driven by a mission.

I don't want to think right now. I want to enjoy the night —it's a special occasion. I want to discover what thoughts have been floating in his head, and I'm positive he is curious about what's been in mine.

Most of all, I want to escape the puzzle pieces of my life that feel scattered, and Wes feels like he could be that escape, even if he is equally a complication.

The elevator doors ping open and we both step in.

"You're right," I respond, stepping into his arms that come out to embrace me. It feels almost like home. "Let's get out of here."

A faint line of victory forms on his mouth at my choice of words before he dips his head down to kiss my cheek slowly and tantalizing, as if he'll suddenly act like a respectable, patient man. Funny, in a way, because neither one of us has patience anymore.

It's finally our night. Because he and I were always inevitable.

WES

How have I managed to keep my lips off of her for the last seventeen minutes? I'm not sure.

"Come on." I indicate with my head to her front door that she just unlocked, my hand never letting hers go.

It was the longest cab ride of my life. Emily looked out the window to avoid my gaze, almost bashful, but I made no mistake that I saw the corners of her mouth tugging up, and I could see her chest moving rapidly from her breathing as she squeezed our interlaced fingers.

Her lips twitch in the faintest of smiles before she pulls me along inside her place and turns the hallway light on as she places the bouquet on the side table.

Yanking her arm to me, I spin her as the door closes and let her back land against the wood. Immediately, I cradle her head and step a leg between her knees to encourage her to part her thighs open as I stare at her sultry smirk. Her eyes dart between my eyes and my mouth.

"You've been thinking about my lips on yours since last time," I remind her as I hook a finger under her chin to tilt her gaze up to my own, and her grin spreads.

"Let's not get cocky now. It was a year ago." Then she looks slightly away with a blush she can't hide. "…But maybe."

"I'm fucking going to devour you, Emmy," I warn her as I move in toward her mouth.

Our lips brush one another's softly before planting together. The spark ignites and our lips collide into a harsh, firm kiss, as if we're both punishing the other for waiting this long. My jacket, which I rested on her shoulders to keep her warm during the ride back, falls to the floor due to her force and the fact that her hands reach to cling to my shoulders.

She's offering back what I give in the strength of my mouth pressing against hers, our own fire blazing between us as warmth spreads within my veins. My hand moves to the back of her head, allowing me to kiss her deeper.

She molds perfectly to my mouth, the subtle taste of wine still on her lips. My tongue meets hers for a reunion, a circling dance, then a stroke, before softening the kiss.

"Wes," she rasps in between our kisses.

"You know how many times I've thought about having you?" I whisper as my mouth brushes along her neck, and I feel her hands work at pulling the fabric of my shirt out of my pants as our mouths reseal together.

Reaching for the hem of her dress with my hands, I begin to skim the silky-soft material up her smooth bare thighs, feeling the heat of her skin get hotter as I move up. My heart skips a beat, as I'm excited that I have her exactly where I want her.

"Wes, please." Her moaning plea awakens every desire I have for this woman to the fullest.

"Have you been this wet all day waiting for me? Were you this excited when you glanced at me all through the wedding ceremony, and were you dripping when I danced with you?" I ask her with my eyes meeting hers.

Her body arches into me as I slowly stroke her again. "I shouldn't answer that." She's trying to tease me in this moment, but her voice is husky.

"Oh, but you will, because I'm the guy who is going to take you the way I wanted to then and the way I want to now. So here is what we're going to do. You're going to wrap your legs around my waist, because I know you want to feel my cock. Am I right?" My thumb stops and I bring it to her lips to rub.

Emily answers my question by bringing one leg up around my waist, and it makes me flash a satisfied smirk. I firmly squeeze her ass as her other leg wraps around me, causing her dress to crinkle around her waist. A gentle whimper escapes her when the bulge of my pants presses against the apex between her legs.

"Fuck, Wes, you are so hard. This is a horrible idea," she mentions with a droll smile as her eyes hood closed and she rocks into me. Clearly her words are not aligning with her actions.

"No, this is a perfect idea," I correct her before our mouths merge together. I walk us in the direction I assume is where her bedroom is with her in my arms, stopping halfway against the wall. "Your pussy is meant to wrap around my cock as I take you. Let me fucking cherish every inch of you," I tell her before she tightens her legs around me and shuts me up with her mouth.

She's straddling me and doesn't let our mouths part until she murmurs against my lips. "You have such a dirty mouth." The hum from the back of her throat sounds like she approves.

We make it to the room and there's enough light from the hall coming in. I sit on the bed and bring her on to my lap.

Her fingers fumble with the buttons of my shirt, heading up, as I undo my buttons going down. Quickly, we whip my shirt off and then I grab the edge of my undershirt and peel it up and off.

Reluctantly, our mouths part and Emily hops off me and the bed to stand. She turns and I come to standing as I eye the zipper on the back of her dress. "I should just rip this off you." I place a soft kiss on her shoulder.

She scoffs a laugh. "Don't do that, I like this dress."

"You like me more," I reply as I help her by pulling the zip down then grabbing the fabric pooled around her waist up and off as she lifts her arms for me. We don't do so elegantly, we have haste.

I pause in our frenzy as I take in a moment to admire her before me, in heels and black lace and no bra. I close our distance with a step and slide my arm around her middle from behind to pull her flush against me, skin to skin. "You are fucking gorgeous. Turn around for me," I whisper into her ear.

She looks back at me and smiles to herself as she pulls her hair to the side and turns slowly in my arms. Our eyes catch and hold with a momentary realization between us that we are finally doing this.

I cradle her head in my hands and tip her head back slightly by gently pulling her hair so she looks up at me as I still stand over her. "Are you on birth control?" I'm selfish when it comes to her. I want to take everything she'll give.

"Yes."

"Good. I need to feel all of you, is that okay?"

"Yeah." Her eyes flutter. "I've never... without."

A slow, subtle smile escapes me. "Guess I'm your first then, and you're mine."

Her fingertips push against my chest in response, with a flirty grin on her face. Her answer is all I need to kiss her mouth possessively because I am a greedy son of a bitch today.

I want to claim her, take her, and make her mine.

My arms wrap around her, and I pull her close and around to throw her to the middle of the bed. The whole move makes her squeal in delight as I crawl over her.

Swirling my tongue around her nipple, she tilts her body up toward me.

"Mmm, that's nice."

"It's only going to get better," I remind her, with my eyes peering up to see her stifling a smile, illuminated by the lights from the hall. I twist her nipple with my fingers as my mouth ravishes the other.

"I believe so," she tells me before she moves to push me onto my back. She comes to her hands and knees. For the last five minutes, it's been constant yanking and pulling of mouths and hands. We both want something from the other and it's making us move chaotically, but perfectly so.

Leaning forward, she runs a trail with her lips up my torso until she lands at my mouth for a quick kiss. I encourage her to press her body on top of me so I can steal more kisses from her mouth, because, God, her tongue feels like heaven and her body entwined with mine makes my cock twitch in excitement.

Her playful look warns me as she slithers down my body, building up all my anticipation for her. Every inch sends an electric current to my cock that needs desperately to feel her.

Emily unbuckles my belt before pulling my pants off then returning to my boxer briefs, and if I was hard before, I just reached a new level of stiff as the tip of her tongue traces the outline of my cock over the fabric, with her eyes gazing up at me for approval.

Gone is the girl who once wanted me to take her gently and slowly in the back of my car. Now is a fucking vixen who seems to be my match in the bedroom.

"You want it, don't you?" I ask as I rake my hands through her hair, and she nods yes.

It takes every fiber inside my soul to move and encourage her to lie down, but I don't want tonight to be about me. Licking and fucking her into the morning is a better present anyhow.

"I need all of this off of you, right now," I whisper as my fingers hook under the lace around her hips. The feeling of her shuddering underneath me reminds me that I have the power in this moment to bring her to her freefall.

Her legs move to kick off the lace.

The grin on my face as I discover her secret treasure must be priceless. My hands guide her ass to tilt up and her lower body to twist so I can view her little tattoo. I can't see exactly what it is, but I think it's small and circular. I growl as I playfully bite.

Emily's hands weave through my hair as she laughs with her head falling back. "You found it."

"Perfect location," I say as I grip her thighs to guide her to lie flat on her back and open wide for me. "But this is the only location I want right now," I warn her before I shimmy down the bed and plant myself between her legs so my mouth can easily kiss her wet slit.

I don't remember her being this loud when she moans, but it's a song my body easily reacts to.

Licking up and down a few strokes, I find her bead that I

circle with the tip of my tongue as one hand caresses her inner thigh.

"So good, so fucking sweet." A mix of arousal, wine, and wedding cake. It's the only explanation I have to how she tastes like a literal dessert.

"I want you," she breathes as her hips roll and her pussy pushes up against my mouth.

She wants me dances around in my head. I like the confirmation.

Quickly bringing my arms under her thighs, I hold her in place. I'm going to make her come and wish she'd begged me a week ago to take her like this.

"Wes, I want to come with you," she coos as her hands palm her perfectly shaped tits.

"You will, but first…"

"Oh, fuck. Right there. So good."

Picking up my rhythm on her clit, I follow her body cues until she is quaking under my mouth, and I don't stop there. I keep my tongue on her until she comes down. And because I don't want to stop touching her—I'll never stop wanting to touch her—I brush my lips along her inner thighs before I slide up the bed to kiss her with my finger pushing inside her warm center to explore.

Her hands cradle my face before she kisses me, and I can feel her tasting her own juices on my mouth which is so fucking hot. The vibration of her moan passes to my mouth as her hand between us grips my cock and begins stroking me. It may just make me explode already.

When she was eighteen, she was willing, and I showed her how to touch me. Her perfect movements now make me believe she never forgot how to touch me, nor will she ever need a lesson from me again, she knows what she's doing.

"You want that, beautiful?" My nose nuzzles to the spot below her ear that I remember she likes.

She licks her lips. "God, yes."

"Say it." I continue my exploration of her warm skin along her neck and shoulder.

"I want your cock, Weston Bay," she answers, slow and sultry, teasing me yet serious.

My finger shifts from her channel before rubbing her one more time to feel what I do to her. She is soaking in arousal.

Hovering over her, my cock slides between her folds, making her sing a sweet hum.

"Look into my eyes, Emmy," I demand and instantly she obeys. "Tell me you want me inside you."

"I want you inside me." The urgency in her tone is borderline desperation and a hint of another meaning that I can't quite figure out. Either way, I love her tone.

Guiding the head of my cock to her entrance, our eyes confirm my next move. I slowly nudge in, causing her to let out a sharp whimper and her nails to sink into my arms, caging her in.

"I've got you," I remind her as I move slower and get enveloped by her slick heat. I study her before kissing her affectionately along her jawline.

"There, Wes. Right there." She begins to move, trying to get me deeper, and I kiss her as I fill her to the brim, so deep that there is nowhere else to go. "We've been waiting too fucking long for this."

We move together before adjusting our position, and she brings her knees out and up with her toes resting on my ass.

"You feel perfect," I confirm what she must already know, before we meet for another passionate kiss. My hands grab her wrists to pin against the mattress above her head. I need to give it to her deep and hard. Prove to her she always has a spot inside me that's for her.

My grunts and her moans mixing with the sound of my cock moving in and out of her pussy should be up for an award best soundtrack.

"Like that. Wes, you feel so perfect in me."

I won't let her forget her words. *Never.*

I pull back gently to swing her leg over to take her from behind in a spooning position.

Our mouths meld together again as we move in sync, hands roaming along her body together as she presses her body against me.

"Deep or fast, baby?"

"Deep…so deep," she says huskily as her arm reaches behind to pull me even closer to her.

I bury my head into the meeting point of her neck and shoulder; we're almost there.

I'm so rooted in her that I have to press my hand on her hip to stop her from moving, to feel how bottomed out I am inside her.

"You want me to come deep inside you?"

"Yes. You want me to come all over your cock?" she answers, and her dirty mouth is a surprise I didn't see coming until tonight.

I return to our rhythm and my senses feel extra sensitive. Everything we're doing together feels heightened, bringing my pleasure level to a whole new realm. It's because it's her. For reasons I've never understood, she's cemented in my brain as the one I want to take a chance with.

"Almost there." I bring my fingers to her clit to bring her with me, and her teeth graze my arm as she moans.

"Me too."

The shooting pressure to my cock and dizziness heightens

when my climax hits. The only way to calm is kiss her as I unload inside her, releasing all the pressure built up over the years, with her shaking around my shaft. I'm not sure if the black spots in my eyesight are me worn out or a sign that we've entered mystical territory.

"Mmmm." Emily snuggles into me by wrapping my arm tighter around her, keeping me inside her, and her angelic sounds confirm that she's satisfied.

She squeezes our interlaced fingers together, and my lips graze along the smooth skin of her shoulder. "Tell me we are doing that again," I request.

11

EMILY

"Don't look at me like that," I warn him as he views me with those sinfully sexy eyes. He's sitting against the big window in my living room with coffee in hand, *shirtless*, and thoroughly satisfied from last night.

I stand safely on the other side of the room with a sheet wrapped around my naked body and a blushing face.

He brings an arm out, indicating for me to walk to him and fall into his embrace. *Tempting.* But I just spent the last three minutes lying in my bed alone and staring at the ceiling trying to bring some sense to my head. It's a difficult task to do after what went down between my sheets during the night.

Waking, I didn't freak out that he wasn't lying next to me, as I could feel he was still here. My apartment is small, and my body has some odd animal sensory around Wes that feels him within a ten-mile radius anyhow.

"Come here," he requests, and that winning grin on his face tells me he isn't going to let me off easy.

I cautiously step a few strides forward, but I'm not ready to commit to running into his arms.

"Your smile is telling me you want to come here, so come here. Don't be shy." He waves me over.

I bite my lip before moving a few more steps. My hesitation is broken when he quickly brings his arm out to encircle around me and pull me to him until I'm standing firmly between his legs where he's sitting on the ledge of the windowsill. And okay, I giggle at his move.

"Morning," he murmurs into my neck at that sensitive spot that is awakening all my nerve-endings.

"*So…* last night happened."

A short laugh escapes him as he drinks casually from his coffee. "It did, and this morning will happen too."

I place a finger against his lips. I need to suggest something logical, yet I feel my teasing voice doesn't want to turn off. "Now, Wes, I'm not sure that is the case. We need to work together."

His eyes go big. "Really? You want to go down that road?"

"It's the smart thing to do."

"Hmm, not sure I agree."

"Last night was… a release, fun… expected. Bound to happen." I bring a shoulder up to my ear.

"You need to have a cup of this disgusting coffee before we talk about this."

"It's not disgusting. It's chicory coffee that you're drinking, and it's full of health and detox benefits. No caffeine," I explain as I watch my fingers draw circles around his chest.

"Okay, this fake coffee won't work, so we go to plan B and head to the shower, then talk," he informs me as he sets the coffee mug down.

"A *shower* shower or a… shower?" I raise a brow as I ask curiously.

"Babe." His voice does something to my ears, my body

too. It sounds smooth and good. Wes's hands land on my ass and he squeezes me over the sheet. "The kind where I get on my knees and worship that little Saturn tattoo on your beautiful ass that I was staring at while you slept this morning." That pulling line of his mouth is my downfall, I swear.

"Jupiter is a hard planet to draw. Saturn has visible rings, and I wanted a planet tattoo." My tone is neutral as I try to steer us away from his one-track mind.

"Okay, fair enough. However, I am surprised by it all, as judging from your post-it wall, I wouldn't strike you as a tattoo person." He flashes his eyes at me.

I roll my eyes. "I'm organized, not uptight, Wes."

"I know." *Ah*, he leans in to nibble my neck a little.

I push him away slightly. "You were looking at my wall?"

"You mean your life plan laid out with the use of post-it notes? Yeah, I did. You have a lot on your agenda for the coming months."

Pointing a finger at him, I use this opportunity to get us on the right track. "Exactly. It's a lot. And adding this," I motion between us, "will complicate it."

"Relax, Emmy." He has the audacity to kiss my forehead so tenderly. "You need a good distraction. It'll help you relax."

I give him knowing eyes. "Let me guess, you are the distraction?"

"So smart you are. Come on," he answers before hoisting me up and throwing me over his shoulder, and even though I protest, there is a giant smile on my face as I wiggle my body.

The next half-hour, he demonstrates to me how he could be the perfect distraction. It involves a lot of tongue action and thrusting. It's effective too, as I completely forgot all thought and begged him to take me in the shower, to which he happily obliged.

Now as I lie on my side on top of my bed in jeans and a t-shirt, I admire the view of him dressing. I'm amused he'll have to make his way home in his clothes from last night.

His phone vibrates, and he grabs it from on top of the dresser and sighs when he reads the screen.

"Everything okay?"

"Yeah, just need to head to Jupiter today to tie up some things," he says as he buckles his belt.

My mind ventures to the list in my head of what I need to do this week. His dad's birthday is next weekend, plus there's a corporate lunch on Wednesday for a small group. I also need to go over the invite list for the opening.

"Don't think about work." He leans down and kisses my forehead, as he knows me too well.

"Listen, Wes, I really think we shouldn't muddle things."

He groans then sits on the bed and touches my leg. "Why is it complicated?" He doesn't sound convinced.

"Because you're my boss, and we need to work together. I literally just came from a company where my colleague slept with the boss, and it didn't end well for anyone."

"Slightly different scenario."

"It's not just that. Your opening is important for you and for me. If people think I got the job purely because I'm sleeping with you then it doesn't help me at all in trying to make Chicago work for me career-wise."

He studies me and he seems to be taking in my words. "So, this is all career related?"

"I-I… don't know." It's a lot of things. Like he is the guy that I would fall in love with since I'm already heading there. Instead, I say, "What about Sadie?"

He now smiles brightly. "I don't think she cares."

"Why do you think that? I never told her about us."

"Nice. An *us* is in your head. But do you think she's that

blind? Plus, I'm sure she will return from her honeymoon in a mood where nobody can do wrong."

"What about you? Don't you want to get settled with your new business?"

I can see his brain working and he must be taking in my words.

"Maybe I need someone to take my mind off all of it." He flashes his eyes at me.

"Fun with you is complicated, Wes," I remind us both of the truth… he could never be just fun to me.

He moves to lean into me and lets his fingertips run along my oblique.

"What about after the opening?"

My eyes dart to his. "I can't think past then."

His tongue makes a gentle clicking sound. "You need to relax, Emmy, then take another look at your plans, as I think they need to be adjusted."

"Wes," I warn him, especially as his finger is roaming.

He kisses my cheek. "We will revisit this topic. I've got to go." He steals a quick peck on my mouth before he gets up and quickly finishes buttoning his shirt before walking to the doorway of my room and pausing. "You're worth the wait, Emmy, but I think we're done waiting." He gives me one last look before leaving.

I fall back onto my bed, slightly aggravated. I wanted Wes last night, I wanted my curiosity of what it would be like with him to be fulfilled, I wanted to *feel*. I also thought getting it out of our system was a good idea. But now that I've gotten a taste of what it would be like with him, I'm not sure of anything anymore.

The feelings for him have always been there, but now I've tangled them in with physical gratification that we are quite good at together. It's all an overpowering emotion now. He is something to me, and he has made it very clear that I am something to him.

It takes a few minutes before I decide to get on with my day. I have laundry to do, need to hit the supermarket, and I should check in with my parents. As I fill my to-go coffee cup in my kitchen, I look at my wall of post-its and notice a few out of place. Strange. Orange is for hobbies, so it's noticeable that there is one in my blue and pink section of work.

Walking closer, my puzzled face relaxes and I laugh. The handwriting on the paper is not from me, but I have a hunch of who it belongs to when I read the notes.

Go to dinner with Wes.

Sleep with Wes… again.

12

WES

"Let's double-check the meat orders for the coming two weeks," I remind Reggie, my chef, as I look over the sheet of supplies he's ordered.

Sitting at a table, I am knee deep in administration. I could do it all from my office, but I like to see everyone busy at work.

Nah, who am I kidding?

No one I hire needs me to guide them, as they all have strong work ethic. Including Emily, who has been avoiding me all morning because her ethics are slightly off-balance and give her the crazy idea that workplace romance is a no-go zone.

She hasn't let her eyes meet my gaze once since sitting on the other end of the restaurant, talking with our graphic designer about party favors.

"I'll check the freezer with Charlie," Reggie mentions, and Charlie nods.

"What about the whiskey supply for your father's event?" Charlie asks.

I chortle a laugh. "Make sure we have about six different

options on hand, all Scottish labels too. If there is one thing he'll criticize, it's our whiskey inventory."

Charlie grins at my remark. "No problem. I'll head to the wholesaler out near Skokie to pick up a few more bottles."

"Sounds good," I confirm as I close my laptop.

"Tomorrow is the staff dinner. I'm really looking forward to having everyone sample the menu, but everyone needs to be critical, though." Reggie smiles proudly, and he should. He is an exceptional chef, and I'm happy I swooped him up before any new restaurant did. He's fairly new to the scene, but his talent is better than any award-winning chef.

"How's the business lunch booked for Thursday looking?" I ask Charlie as he scrolls his tablet.

"Emily said we'll just change the colors of the flowers to match their logo, and she already let Reggie know the extra dietary requirements and confirmed number of attendees."

"Would never have thought to change flower colors." I tilt my had to the side as I think about that. "Alright, I think we're all up to date. Oh, Reggie, do you have the final menu for my dad's thing?" I ask before taking a drink of my water.

"Yeah, Emily already gave me her input last week," he answers as he gets up to head back to the kitchen.

"Oh, did she?" I look at Emily across the room who's laughing with that elated smile, and the pink in her cheeks matches the peach color of her dress.

"I will check in with her then," I call out to Reggie as he walks away.

Quickly, I glance at my phone and have to laugh when I see Cole texted me.

COLE

Did your post-wedding festivities match that of the bride & groom's? Mine sure as hell did.

ME

I wouldn't expect anything less from you.

Did the maid of honor end up happy?

He inserts a winking emoji.

I don't kiss and tell.

Except we all witnessed your foreplay
during toasts and dinner.

That comment makes me let a laugh out, as there is some truth to that.

Are you going to tell me how your night
ended up?

Another day. Want to meet for a drink this
week? Since Logan is on his off-the-grid
honeymoon in Wisconsin of all places & my
sister is annoying the hell out of me about
dating then it seems like you are my only
option.

What a douche he is sometimes, but I know it's all light-hearted.

Truly touched by your honesty. Maybe.
Need to see how my week goes.

You mean if Emily wants round two? Or
wants to trade up and give me a call?

Again, I know he's only messing with me, yet just the thought of it makes me boil.

He inserts a tiger emoji, and I shake my head at his tendencies to be an ass.

Sliding my phone back into my pocket, I glance over at Emily and Layla, the graphic designer we use and who happened to be at my sister's wedding.

I decide to head over their way and throw on my charming smile as I approach them, and I overhear Layla encouraging Emily.

"You will have so much fun freelancing. I have no complaints," Layla says as she places her tablet back into her bag.

"Hey, ladies, can I join in on the fun?" I ask as I slide into a chair around the table.

Emily gives me a tight-lipped smile and crosses her arms, plus her eyes give the I'm-on-to-you look.

"Layla has some amazing designs for the party favors that we'll give for the opening. So I told her to go ahead and order a hundred and fifty," Emily explains as she taps her notebook in a steady beat with her pen.

"I leave it with you. What are the favors?" I wonder.

The corner of Emily's mouth tilts up. "A surprise."

I could show her a few surprises if she would let me.

"Your sister had a beautiful wedding. I already saw the photos on a few blogs." Layla smiles as she looks between Emily and me.

"Thanks. I guess we didn't get much time to talk at the wedding. I only spoke with Josh briefly," I mention.

"It's okay, you were on big-brother duties. I was just

telling Emily that she shouldn't be afraid to start solo," Layla tells me.

"You gave me some good advice, thanks," Emily says and gives Layla a warm and genuine smile, the smile that I'm dying to be on her face when she turns in my direction.

"I'm not a number person, but I'm sure one of the guys could look at your business plan," Layla suggests as she zips her bag.

Quickly I offer, "More than happy to."

Layla nudges Emily's arm. "See, a true Prince Charming." Layla flashes me a wink.

Leaning forward, I rest my arms on the table. "Hey, Layla, wasn't Josh your boss when you two got together?"

Emily gives me the death stare and her bottom lip drops slightly. Her eyes even bulge subtly.

Layla looks between Emily and me and can't help but looked entertained. She knows me well enough that she's on to what I'm up to. "Why, yes. Josh was my boss when we decided to give it a whirl and then unexpectedly got pregnant," she confirms with a hint of humor, but all completely true.

"Sounds like a winning formula." I grin as I stare at Emily who looks like she's considering options of how to kill me discreetly.

Standing, Layla throws her bag over her shoulder. "In the end it was. Sorry I can't stay for dessert, but Josh is working from home and our child decided there's no sleep for the wicked."

"Thanks for everything." Emily smiles.

"Sure, I'll e-mail you later when I know when the items will be delivered." Layla waves us off and leaves.

I stand up then slide into the chair next to Emily, ensuring that I pull the chair close to her to make her visibly tremble.

"Wes," she purrs and makes a point to move her chair a few inches away from me.

"So that winning formula sounds good, minus the unplanned pregnancy," I tease her, and her eyes roll to me.

She brushes past my quip. "Something you need?"

I stare at her, and I know she won't budge so decide to actually talk work. "Reggie mentioned you finalized my dad's menu."

"I did." She opens her notebook and pulls out her phone to swipe to an e-mail with the list of food.

"I really hope your notebook has a page dedicated to a few dishes that we could try," I mention casually as I lean back in my chair.

"Now, now, Wes, we know that wouldn't be workplace appropriate," she taunts me without even looking at me—the woman's hidden skill.

"Least we agree on something." I adjust my seating position so I can look at her phone screen.

"Thanks for disrupting my post-it wall." I'm happy she's bringing it up, because I definitely don't plan on brushing the other night under the rug.

"I will destroy your notebook too," I promise.

Emily really doesn't want to smile, but she can't fight it as she throws me side-eye.

"Let's look at this menu, okay?" I suggest as my fingers make her screen zoom in.

She clears her throat slightly and straightens her posture. "Right, so I just asked Reggie to take some of your main menu items and make it slightly healthier, and then for dessert we have two options. A healthy one and blueberry cheesecake, because Sadie mentioned that—"

"It's my parents' favorite? Yeah."

"Exactly, I e-mailed your dad's secretary to check if we

should do a seating arrangement, and she sent me the names and plan, so I will have place cards. Your mother and I briefly spoke at the wedding too, so I think it'll all be alright. Sadie won't be back from her honeymoon yet, so I think it's just…" Emily is afraid to say it.

"Me and the pack of wolves?"

"I'll make sure everything is taken care of, so you don't need to worry about a thing," she promises and touches the top of my hand to comfort me.

"Thanks."

We stare into each other's eyes, and we get a little lost as I reach up to trap her hand between my own.

"Really can't persuade you for a quickie up in my office?" I flash my eyes at her.

I love her blushing face; it's the perfect shade of pink and warm. I've now seen her this way next to me and under me, and one of those ways is better than the other.

Before she can answer, she nearly jumps in her seat like my hands became a stove to burn her, and Emily nervously twists some hair around her finger. "Oh, hey there, Reggie."

Reggie smiles and places a plate of dessert in front of her. "For the ladies."

Emily beams and immediately grabs a fork. "This looks *amazing*. Layla had to go, but I am all for having two. Is it really marshmallow? The smores bomb sounds like my dream," Emily gushes, and my mind remembers the very first time I kissed her with remnants of marshmallow on her lips.

"Absolutely. Graham cracker crumble, a layer of cheese-cake made from marshmallow and cream cheese, melted chocolate, and then extra marshmallows blazed with a torch. *Bon appetit*," Reggie says before heading back to the kitchen.

I watch Emily place a forkful of dessert into her mouth and I feel like she is slowly sucking the fork to play with me.

"Mmm, now this is something you could persuade me to do anything for." The wicked look she gives me is dirty, and I'm all for that.

"Say no more, let's go. I have no problem going against health and safety rules anywhere in this place."

She laughs and stakes the fork into the dessert again before pulling up a giant piece of the crumble dessert. Then she surprises me and guides the fork to my mouth where I ensure our eyes hold as I slowly suck the fork.

Emily is actually feeding me in my own restaurant, and suddenly it feels like this place is now complete.

The moment she realizes what she's doing, she stops and drops the fork like a hot iron.

"I most definitely should not be feeding my boss in public."

I angle my body to her and lean in slightly. "And in private?"

"Wes, let's revisit this topic in a few weeks." She's staying firm on her standpoint.

There is a long silence between us as she plays with the food on her plate.

"So, you want me to forget about the other night and hit pause? I thought that was your disgusting coffee talking." I'm checking what exactly she wants, as people don't fuck one another the way we did a handful of times only to forget it.

She makes a hushing sound and scans the room. "Not here. Can we save this conversation for another time?"

"Sure, but just tell me you don't regret it." I sound vulnerable right now. This woman must know she has the ability to bring me to my knees.

Her eyes meet mine and her face softens. "No way. I just know that if we end up in bed together now that I'll only want more."

EMILY

Looking over the long table, I'm proud of my simple and quick turnaround for the staff dinner. Wes seemed to think we would all just have a casual dinner, to which I scoffed at that suggestion. I set the table, left little thank-you notes on everyone's plate from Wes—he just doesn't know it. Then I added some silver confetti to the table to make it more festive.

I let out an exhale as I bounce my shoulders in accomplishment. Looking at my phone on top of my notebook that I'm holding, I see that I have a new e-mail from Layla. It's just a quick one with a recommendation of a bank to use for small business. My bank on the East Coast is regional so it won't be ideal for Chicago.

My phone vibrates in my hand, and I see it's Ruby. Since Sadie is on her honeymoon, Ruby and I are in more contact.

"Hey, can't talk long, I'm at work," I answer and look around at all the staff arriving, so I walk a few steps to the corner.

"Ooh, nice, does Wes have you bent over his desk yet or

do you just reserve that for post-wedding festivities?" Ruby retorts with her typical ability to speak her mind.

"Ruby," I warn under my breath. "Not now, and what would make you say that?"

"I saw you and Wes leave together. Sadie is going to *love* this." I hear Ruby smiling on the other end.

"No you don't. You are not bothering her on her honeymoon."

"Yep. There's that confirmation I was looking for. I have something to tell her." She sounds like a six-year-old on the playground.

I give a low growl, aware someone can overhear me. "Ruby, please can you let it go?"

"Relax. Your secret is safe with me. Does this mean that you and Weston boy are finally happening? Only took a solid six years," she tells me, and it reminds me that, in a moment of weakness after she witnessed my public indiscretion, I spilled the beans that it hadn't been the first time.

I shake my head, as I'm getting slightly aggravated by her. "He is my boss, and I need to focus on getting settled back in Chicago."

"Hmm, you sound a little stressed. I'm sure he can help you with that."

"What the hell? I can't stay in this conversation. Why did you call?"

"Whoa, touchy. Okay, and you're right." She lets out a breath. "I hope it works out for you, Emily. Maybe he's part of your life plans but you just forgot to plan him in." I hear the seriousness in her tone, and her words seem almost wise and maybe even true.

"That's…maybe a thought," I admit. "Look, I should go," I reply as I look across the room and see Wes chatting with one of the college-aged waiters. Wes touches his shoulder, as if he's encouraging him, and that natural smile sends a wave of warmth through me—and the smile isn't even for me.

My melancholy feeling is interrupted by Ruby. "Do you think we can meet up soon? I kind of need an ear."

"Oh God, who did you sleep with?" is my first thought, and I speak aloud and realize I wasn't quiet enough. A few heads look my way, including Wes's, with furrowed lines formed on his forehead.

"I didn't. It's more complicated… or maybe not. Can we just meet?"

Quickly I mutter into my phone, "Sure, I'll text you tomorrow," then hang up as everyone returns to their conversations.

Looking at Wes, I feel like his eyes just sparkled at me. Sometimes I wonder if that's only ever for me. Breaking our gaze, I go to my bag resting on a bar stool and put my notebook back. Kimmy, the blond-haired beauty who is a waitress, asks me what I would like to drink, and I just tell her the same as her. No clue what it is.

Bad mistake. Terrible mistake.

Colossal.

During appetizers of burrata and calamari, I'm in my own world. Purposely, I sit as far away from Wes as possible. I did it for years so it should be easy, right?

Wrong.

Ruby's words keep sinking into my brain. It becomes an overbearing thought, further induced by the cosmopolitans that keep getting topped up in my hand while I pretend to listen to Kimmy talk about belly-dancing yoga.

Despite drinking water when I remember, I feel, well… loose.

"Another round everyone? We're all off the clock," Charlie announces to everyone with a grin, and the response is a whistle and some cheers. Then quickly new bottles of wine are being passed around.

I'm relieved when the fantastic chimichurri steak is placed in front of me to soak up some of my thoughts floating around about plans and Wes.

Kimmy nudges my arm. "He is so hot, isn't he?"

This wakes me up in full force.

"Who?" I double-check.

"Wes. He's single, and that's a damn shame. I wonder if I could do something about that if we all go to a club after this."

I choke on the taste of vodka in my cosmopolitan. "Uhm. He is your boss."

"And? The last place I worked; everyone was hooking up with someone."

"You know, I don't think he's that single." It comes out slightly hitched.

"Do you know something? Oh yeah, Reggie mentioned you and Wes go way back."

My palm flies up to quickly defend myself. "Not like that. His sister and I are best friends."

She studies me as she downs the last of her drink. "So, you didn't get this job because you and he had a thing?"

My head shakes no at an unusually fast speed to correct her.

"Hmm, that's a shame. We could totally have made a social media reel about sleeping with the boss to create some buzz for the place."

Before this conversation can go further south, the sound of a knife clinking against glass brings everyone's attention to Wes who is standing at the head of the table.

"Okay, everyone. Happy to see everyone is having a good

time. Just wanted to quickly say thank you for doing everything to help get ready for the launch. I think it's going to pay off, as it seems we're breaking social media the last day or two. People are e-mailing to ask for invites, and even the old-school Trib newspaper wants a seat at the opening," Wes sincerely tells everyone, and I can see he's happy. Naturally content.

"I'm glad we could just take a moment to let go a little before we dive deep into the first weeks of Jupiter. Thanks again, everyone." He tilts his glass up, as does everyone else. Wes quickly glances at me and gives me a wink, and I feel something in the area of my heart tug.

It's not just a tug, it's full-on pulling the doors open.

When Wes turns his attention back to Charlie, I speak to Reggie over the table to distract myself. "I'm excited to have the smores bomb again. Good choice putting that on the menu. It'll become a fan favorite for sure."

"Really?" He grins proudly.

"Of course, marshmallow is a powerful ingredient."

"Funny. It wasn't even on the menu until last week," Reggie casually replies as he drinks from his iced water.

"Oh? What changed?"

"Wes asked me to add something with marshmallow to the menu."

The cosmo that I intended to sip turns to a gulp.

Weston Bay is in full-on pursuit, and his moves aren't that bad.

———

"ARE you sure you guys are okay?" I ask one of the waiters as he waves me off, and he moves to close the door with a very tipsy Kimmy in the backseat of the cab.

"Don't worry, I'll get her home. She's roommates with my sister."

I want to say that is exactly why I worry, because friends of the sister sometimes do something to guys, but I let it go.

The door to the cab closes and they drive off.

Holding my phone high and into eyesight, I check the taxi app, but Weston's hand grabs my phone.

"Let me make sure you get home," he tells me as he stands there on the sidewalk looking determined.

"It's okay, Wes, I've *so* got this."

"Humor me." The streetlights highlight his authoritarian look.

"No. I don't need more people thinking I'm sleeping with the boss." I point a finger at him.

He glances around then back at me. "Almost everyone is gone. Only Charlie is inside with Reggie, so I'm not taking no for an answer," he says as a cab drives up to the curb, and Wes opens the door. His arm gestures to the backseat like a display.

I grumble low, but I slide into the backseat with Wes following me.

"I'm not drunk," I clarify as I cross my arms.

"I know, but you're just buzzed enough that I know this could get good." He nudges my arm with his own.

"No, because you are not coming home with me." I give him a pointed look.

"Sure, Scout's honor." He has the audacity to salute me.

"I'm *totally* on to your games."

"Oh, the truth card is out tonight, but what games do you think I'm playing?"

My hand waves between us. "That trip to the farm, the dessert menu of your establishment, very good sex, and those little pupils in your eyes that have some magical sparkle dust or something."

Wes slides closer to me. "Only very good? Not excellent?"

I pinch his arm, but I have to smile. "Keep a solid personal distance from me, please."

He slides closer, and his body warmth hits me, along with his sharp masculine scent. A pulsing feeling hits me between the legs. Even with too many cosmos, my inner walls decide they can still contract with need right now.

"You are a little bossy right now. Is that what you want? To reverse the roles?" he asks as he brings an arm to rest behind me on the seat and his nose nuzzles my hair.

"No. I will not kiss you. I will not fuck you. I will wait until you are no longer my boss before we have any conversation of this regard," I list.

His upper lip curves up. "Here's the thing, Emmy." He places his hand on my knee and draws up my dress slightly with his finger. "We've both been waiting way too long for this thing between us, so why deprive us of even more time?"

The feeling of his lips caressing my earlobe before adding in a little nibble with his teeth makes me shudder.

The taxi makes a sharp turn and I fly into Wes's arms which makes him flash me a winning grin. "Talk about the stars falling into my lap."

I playfully slap him but don't leave his embrace. "Stop being somewhat swoony."

"I will do no such thing," he says as his fingers begin to stroke my hair, and the move makes me instantly relax.

"Mmm, that's nice." I gently close my eyes as I take in the sensitivity that the feeling his fingers brings to me. That plus the alcohol makes my head spin slightly.

"Rest your eyes. I promise when we get there that I won't

carry you inside then lay you in bed and make you come before you beg me to stay." He is so neutrally toned when he tells me that.

"Fine. You promise," I remind him.

A calm spreads through the cab as we say nothing, but the vague sounds of an old Augustana song plays. It all amplifies my whirling and equally free feeling. Not a care in the world in this moment.

"What's three times three, Emmy?" he asks as he continues to stroke my hair and arms, but my eyes stay closed.

"Nine." I surprise myself on that one in this moment.

"What's the capital of Idaho?"

"Boise," I reply.

"Cubs or Sox?" He continues his questioning to see how sober I am.

"Cubs, of course," I shoot back.

He chuckles softly. "You're going to be perfectly okay," he assures me.

"Sure. I just need to find a way to ensure I don't fall more in love with my boss," I lazily say, but a moment later, my eyes shoot open when I realize what I said. In a flash, I am sitting up and sliding as far away from Wes as possible, with my cheeks flushed.

His tongue runs along the inside of his cheek as he tries to contain his grin, and at the very moment, the cab comes to a stop.

"Saved by the taxi driver's speeding." He clucks his mouth as he indicates to my apartment building, and his eyes never leave me.

I can't muster any words, and I'm frozen as Wes tactfully leans across me to open my door. So close but not touching. "See? Complete gentleman dropping you off and not carrying you inside to lay you on your bed and make you come so you fall more for him."

I roll my eyes. "You misheard." I blink several times.

"Sure, I didn't hear anything and will not bring it up again," he says, playing along.

A disgruntled sound escapes me as I slide out of my seat to standing. Turning around, I face Wes who is following me out of the cab.

"Wait, what are you doing? You said you would be an upstanding gentleman who drops me off?"

He buttons his blazer. "Yeah, so my manners tell me to walk you to your door. Remember, around you, I seem to have them." He leans over to the passenger front window to speak to the driver.

My guess is to ask him to wait, which is ridiculous, as by the time Wes goes inside with me and up the three floors, then I know when we're at my door, he'll try his luck. Or maybe he'll look at me that way that makes me light up inside, then we'll have an overbearing silence before he touches me so innocently and wishes me goodnight…

"Wait!" *Oh no.* "Just stay." Yep, my mind thinks this is a horrible idea to add to confusion, but my body and mouth don't agree… at all.

Wes cocks his head to the side with a smug look. "So, *you* are asking me to stay?"

"I mean, it's late and let's not waste the driver's time." I roll my eyes, tap my foot, and pretend my reasoning is logical.

Wes says something to the driver before turning to me, stepping closer to me, eyeing me like prey. "Let's get you to bed."

My fingertips hit his chest to stop him worming his way closer to me. "Only sleep. You will be gone by the time I wake up, and there will be no additional activities of the naked variety," I inform him rather confidently.

He looks at me, amused. "Fine, but is cuddling out of the picture?"

That sounds kind of enjoyable. "I mean, I guess that could be innocent enough."

"Any more ridiculous boundaries for this evening that I shall obey since I'm crazy about you too?" That subtle smirk illuminated by the streetlight elevates a feeling close to my heart and makes the corners of my mouth twitch.

My shoulder slants up. "I guess. I mean, you don't *need* to wear a shirt to bed. You normally don't anyway."

His response is that velvety chuckle, so deep, and it tickles me in all the right places.

This is a fucking lost cause. My willpower is zero.

Yet to my damn surprise, the man has his own tricks up his sleeve. He actually obeys everything I request. Even in bed, when I casually press back to try and rub against him, he behaves.

I toss and turn a few times from frustration.

"Everything okay there, Emmy?" He pretends to be concerned, knowing damn well what I want.

"You make me so confused and I don't think clearly. You are so damn distracting." I'm slightly frustrated.

"The best kind, baby." He grins before turning the side table light off.

We settle into a spooning position, and although the first few minutes are rather treacherous with want, we both fall into a deep sleep until I wake in the morning to find that Wes actually listened to my request and left before I woke.

Much to my disappointment.

● 14

WES

I look around Jupiter, and everyone is busy setting up for the event tonight—my dad's work dinner. It's the last chance for him to have all his law partners grovel at his feet before retirement. Praise him for recovering from his minor heart attack and kiss up so they may be next to take over lead of the firm. And in a moment of insanity, I agreed he could have this event here.

Jupiter looks good tonight; dark navy-blue flowers in jars with gold ribbon to match the cloth napkins with a band to hold them in place. It's sophisticated and perfect for a corporate gathering.

My eyes search for Emmy and spot her instantly, talking with Charlie as they examine the bottles of whiskey on display behind the bar. The black dress she's wearing looks like it would slide right off her if I unzipped it, and since I know it'll cross her mind, then I'll taunt her at some point tonight. She shakes her wrist full of bracelets as she speaks, and I quickly steal a glance from her.

I've been a well-behaved soul, and since the other night, I haven't brought up what she said, since hearing it was confirmation enough. Now I will just have to be patient and leave things in her court. Of course, Emmy, being her, hasn't brought it up either, and in fact, pretends nothing ever happened. Avoidance is sometimes her tactic, which only means it is a big deal.

That thought alone briefly lifts my spirits, and I smile to myself. It makes tonight feel like a piece of cake, but the sight of Charlie and Emily still in deep discussion reminds me that tonight is anything but.

I walk to them and immediately their heads perk up at me.

"Everything okay?" I ask, glancing between them.

"Yeah, one of the whiskey bottles dropped and broke. Emily was telling me she thought that was one of your dad's favorites—" Charlie begins.

"Or at least I remember your parents drinking it some-times at their house," she finishes the explanation.

"The limited edition Kilchoman?" My question is twined with fear.

"It was an accident when one of the guys was stocking the glasses," Charlie says.

My hand rakes through my hair. "It's a fuck-up that we don't need right now." I'm annoyed and furious.

In the corner of my eye, I see Emily and Charlie speaking to one another through facial expressions.

"It's just a bottle," he mentions again.

Normally I wouldn't care, as it is just one of the many whiskey selections, but did it have to be the bottle that I *know* my dad will ask if I have on hand? Then he will give me one of his many judgmental looks for the evening when I say no.

"Everyone needs to be more careful," I snap.

"And you need to settle down," Charlie shoots back.

"Guys." Emily holds her hand up then turns to Charlie as

she gently touches my arm. "Will you excuse us for a minute?"

"Gladly," Charlie responds.

Emily gives Charlie a closed-mouth smile as she gently tugs me to indicate that I should follow her. We head around the corner to the hallway to the kitchen and she abruptly stops before she pivots with her full attention on me.

"Wes." Her tone tells me she is about to lecture me.

I can only sigh in frustration.

"I know why you're acting this way, but everyone else doesn't. So right now, you look like the jackass boss." Her eyes give me a scolding look as her hand rests on her hip.

"What? It's just a normal day and everyone needs to step it up," I answer as I look around to see if I can get a glimpse into the kitchen to see that they're working hard.

It's only when the warmth of her hand squeezing my upper arm hits me that I fully focus on Emily and know she just pressed that button in me where I can let down a wall or two. She gets me.

"It's not just a normal day. Not to you," she tells me and gives me a comforting look.

I can only nod gently.

"Wes… you and your dad have the oddest relationship. Equal parts strained and supportive—"

I interject right there. "He isn't supportive."

A surprised scoff escapes her beautiful mouth. "Really? Maybe he'll never fly a message across the sky, but there is something you must realize if you haven't already. Even though he doesn't say it, he chose to have his special dinner here. You know why, right?"

"So he can rip me to pieces."

She steps closer to me, and her other hand meets my shoulder, then she playfully shakes me. "No, silly. So he can show you off. Show this place off. And I think Psychology 101 tells me that people only do that when they're proud."

Her smile spreads as she watches me take in and consider her words.

"Trying to make me feel better?" I step dangerously close to her, and I'm tempted to wrap my arms around her then press her against the wall.

"You don't need me for that. You've got this. And don't worry, I have a solution so your dad won't even notice that his favorite whiskey isn't here." She flashes her eyes at me, and her palms rub along my arms.

"Arsenic?"

She laughs at my humor. "No, but trust me."

Our eyes hold and I have no doubt in my mind. "I always do."

Her head tilts in an angle and for a second I get excited that she's preparing herself to kiss me. A quick one that no one would see but would send me to a place of Zen.

Instead, she steps back and looks over my shoulder.

"Wes, can you come check out front?" Charlie calls out from behind me and a slight feeling of dread spreads again, but this time, slightly more bearable.

———

ONLY TEN MINUTES in and the rumble of laughter fills the room, men who have ties at work and at home. A constant pattern of legal jokes and mentioning what their wife—who is hanging off their arm—has been up to.

"The place looks good, Weston, it's beautifully set for tonight. Did Emily help you?" my mother asks as she sips from her glass of dry white wine, her eyes scanning the room.

"She did. She's around here somewhere," I answer, and I'm surprised my radar hasn't instantly found her.

"Wonderful. The seating arrangements are perfect too."

"Yeah, she asked Tracy for input." I smirk at my mother for the reminder that my father's secretary helped with this occasion.

But my mother is a pro and doesn't flinch. "I would think so. This will be a perfect occasion for your father to re-energize the firm since he's fully recovered."

Scratching my cheek, I appreciate her effort to make this as normal of an evening as possible. "Have you heard from Sadie?" I return the effort to make small talk.

My mother smiles as she sets her glass on the bar top. "Of course not, she's on her honeymoon. I would hope she is in contact with nobody. You only get one honeymoon."

"Sure," I say rather dryly, and I give a double take when I see Emily talking with my father and a few of the partners from his firm.

"I will catch up with you after dinner. Hope you enjoy the meal." I touch my mother's arm briefly.

"You're not joining us?"

"Maybe."

Quickly I walk to the other side of the room and arrive to the circle, where Emily clearly has everyone wrapped around her finger.

"I know your loyalty is to Scottish brands, but we have this little teaser that I know you will love, including Swedish whiskey—the latest from Mackmyra—and then we have an Australian whiskey, and finally whiskey from Matchbox out in Colorado." Emily presents the small trays with three little whiskey glasses that are perfectly shaped and sized on a dessert plate.

The men all get to work on trying their first whiskey.

She steps back to me, causing our bodies to touch, and she mutters under her breath as she smiles, "See? I told you, crisis averted."

I speak low as I lean into her space. "Where did all of this come from?"

"The bottle broke a few hours ago, so I sent Charlie to the whiskey store in the Gold Coast while I went to Water Tower Place to grab some glasses."

"Ah, so you used your sorcery to surprise me." It makes me grin.

"No. I left my magic wand in my bedroom drawer next to the rope, so I'm just plain awesome," she retorts then glances over her shoulder at me.

She's my girl. No doubt about that.

"Weston." Because, of course, my father's voice has to break the mood. "Come here and tell us about the history of this place." He reaches a hand out, like a slap on the back is just the way he and I roll.

Sure. I'll play along.

"It's good to see you, Son," he announces in front of everyone, because heaven forbid hell freezes and he tells me in private.

"Busy times," one of my dad's law partners says. "Your sister's wedding and now opening this place. I used to come here when it was with the old owners, and this new look really rejuvenates the place." I remember Mr. Connor from over the years.

"It was a hell of a remodel, but I'm happy with the end result, and you'll love the menu," I proudly respond.

"If it's anything like the whiskey menu then we are in for a good night," my father adds, and I have to glance at him to double-check that aliens haven't kidnapped him then switched bodies.

I keep my professional charm on. "We have a solid wine selection to accompany each dish on the menu this evening, and we kept it as local as possible."

"Wonderful, let's all head to the table perhaps," my father suggests, and the men agree.

As we make our way to the table, my father asks me in low tone, "You are joining us for dinner, of course."

I'm amused by him this evening, that's for sure. "Maybe. But I do need to work," I mention and wonder if this is where he'll ask me to stay because he really wants me there.

Instead, he replies, "Good man. Solid work ethic."

———

Sitting on my chair, my feet rest on my desk, a glass of scotch hanging from my hand. A faint knock on my door doesn't break me from my daze, staring at the ceiling.

"Come in," I say before taking another sip from the liquid gold.

"You're going to hide in here?" Emily's voice awakens a need inside of me to snap out of my mood.

Sliding my feet off the desk, I return to a normal sitting position and allow my eyes to follow her slow glide in my direction.

"Not hiding. Just needed a break," I try to justify as she comes to sit on my desk.

"What? You don't have interest in retirement plans and court caseloads?" She feigns shock as her fingers touch my hand that's holding the scotch, encouraging me to give her the glass.

"Are they almost done?"

I like how she confidently takes my glass to sip without

asking, with her eyes never leaving me. "Still need to get dessert."

That news makes me sigh, and I know I need to go downstairs to make another appearance and join everyone for another round of drinks.

Her leg moves to coax my knees to part open, which I gladly oblige, but I have to give her a puzzled look. "Is there something *you* need?"

Quickly, she moves to straddle me in the chair. "Yes," she rasps.

My eyes give her the once-over before trailing a line up to her eyes. "What would that be?"

"Something to relax you, because I know how much this night is getting to you, and it shouldn't." Her arms slide around my neck, and suddenly my night is looking up.

"I thought you said you don't want to sleep with your overly handsome boss that you are *absolutely* falling for."

Her fingers play with the loose buttons at the top of my dress shirt. The way she looks at me, the manner she touches me, the connection between our bodies makes a smile tilt on her lips.

"I don't think I ever had a chance at that theory, and I think I need to distract you more," she gives me a sultry warning.

In a flash, she plants her mouth on mine, and her kiss makes up for the last few days when we should have been doing this. She gives me her all with lips and tongue. The moan from the back of my throat is a near rumble as I move to pull her closer to my body and return everything she gives.

Her dress rides up to her waist and her pelvis rolls over my quickly emerging and satisfied-at-this-change-of-events erection happening in my pants.

Grabbing the back of her head, I hold her firmly in place as I inch back slightly. "What are you doing?"

"Giving you something to look forward to, because I won't let this be a bad day for you."

Her answer makes my lips twitch, as it is an answer only Emmy would say. "Let's get out of here."

She chortles at my response. "You still have guests downstairs, and we can't leave together, otherwise everyone will know I'm sleeping with my boss." That standpoint, she seems to still be firm on, and I kind of get it, but not enough for me to question it right now.

"So you're sleeping with me now?" I smirk, and she gently shakes her head, amused. "You'll wait for me at my place? You obviously know where I live and which room is my bedroom, but finally I get to witness you in my bed. I'll give you the key." I stroke her cheek and I love how my thumb feels against her soft skin.

"Then I'll finish up here and use the key to wait for you." She licks her lips, and her voice almost sounds shy which is crazy since she oozes confidence tonight.

A thousand possibilities of how she will be waiting for me pop up in my head and it makes me growl into the base of her neck as I lift us up and out of the seat. Then I set her on my desk with my hands moving to hold her hips in place to encourage her to keep her legs wrapped around my middle.

"And if I want a distraction right now?" I ask as I begin to place kisses up her neck.

Her hands splay against my chest, and she considers what to do.

"You want me on my knees?"

"Fuck yes. Let me see your gorgeous red lips wrapped around my cock." In excitement, I run kisses along her jawline as I cradle her head.

"You want me to suck you until I taste you on my tongue?" she whispers.

"Emmy," I hum before slamming a kiss over her mouth.

Reluctantly pulling away, she informs me of the obvious. "I need to look respectable when I go back downstairs and face your father. Not like his son just fucked me senseless."

But she grins, and I love that. That sentence also buzzes a thrill in me for some reason.

I rub my thumb over her mouth. "Fuck, that didn't help my imagination. I quite like that idea."

She grabs my wrists so I don't wander farther over her body. "I have already been away long enough, but I'll be waiting for you." She gives me a quick peck on my lips.

I don't let her hand go until the very last moment when our distance is too much. "On my bed. You'll be waiting on my bed," I inform her, and I think she likes my insistence.

15

EMILY

"Hey there, boss." I put on my best sexy voice as I lie in the middle of Wes's bed on my stomach with my feet up in the air. Of course, I ensured we're ready to go so I took my dress off but left the black lace panties and dark heels on.

Wes stares at me with his mouth gaped open as he stands in the doorway to his bedroom, already beginning to unbutton his shirt. "Emmy, this is such a perfect image that I almost feel bad that I'm about to ravage you in zero-point-three seconds."

"Don't feel bad, I have plans of my own."

He throws his shirt off and begins to stride his way to the bed as he unbuckles his belt.

My fingers walk on top of his dark gray duvet. "You know last time I was in this bed, you weren't physically here," I remind him of the fact that I once slept in his bed when he was away.

"That's a damn shame." He whips his pants off, and his knees landing on the bed causes the mattress to dent as he slowly crawls to me. "Was I on your mind when you touched yourself in my bed?"

The back of his long finger brushes up my spine causing my clit to pulse and for my breath to grow shallow. "Yes," I admit.

Wes lies on his side and props his head up with his arm as more of his fingers caress my skin then trace the line of my shoulder blade.

"Show me how you made yourself come in *my* bed, wishing I was there." His request turns me on and my nipples tingle from want, especially when his fingers brush along the sides of my breast against the mattress.

Slowly and with purpose, I roll to my back with our eyes not parting. That is until he leans down to place a soft kiss on the flesh of my breast before meeting my lips. His kiss turns hungry as his hand turns my jaw to his direction.

"Touch yourself. I want to watch," he requests against my lips.

He peeks down when my hands move to my breasts and squeeze then rub my nipples between my thumbs and fingers, but it's his eyes on me that arouses me.

"Like this?" I ask for approval in a nearly pouty voice.

"Just like that," he confirms before his fingers join me. "You wished I was touching you?"

"I imagined what it would be like with you," I breathe out. I've imagined a lot of things with him.

"So you played with your perfect tits then touched your pussy, wishing I was there?"

My hand travels down and my fingers sneak under the lace to glide between my folds. "Mmmhmm."

"Keep touching yourself, I like watching you. But it will be the last time tonight," he warns me as his fingertips brush along my stomach, and his eyes are fixated on my fingers playing with my clit. "Only I will make you come after this."

My fingers rub circles around my bead, causing me to moan. Immediately, Wes takes over and touches me with the perfect rhythm, making me feel like I'm already about to come.

"Christ, Emmy, you are soaking. How long have you been this way?" he asks as he slips a finger inside me, causing me to gasp softly in surprise.

"All night."

"I need to come all over and in you tonight." His words are dirty, but his delicate kiss on my forehead as he says it is a contrast.

"I wouldn't complain." I throw him a humorous look before I bite my bottom lip and my hand reaches for his hard cock begging to be free from his boxer briefs.

I squeeze and stroke through the fabric as my eyes hood closed from the intensity of Wes's fingers moving between my legs.

Tonight, I want it to be all about him, to take his mind off everything. I want our own little world between these walls where nothing needs to make sense.

"Let me taste you, Wes," I say as I grab his wrist to stop him touching me. I'll prolong my first orgasm if it means that I can please him.

He groans but reluctantly obliges before he lies down.

Quickly, I move and sit on my knees and fling my hair to the side. Hooking my fingers under his boxer briefs, I peer up to see the anticipation on his face. My eyes don't leave his as I pull the fabric down, and I shimmy back to station myself between his legs.

I flash him a knowing grin as my hand firmly grips his base and my lips cover the head of his cock. My tongue swirls the drops of his pre-cum on his tip, the subtle bitter taste that I like because it's his. Then I lower my mouth, with my tongue whirling around his smooth skin, as I thrust him into my mouth.

I love when his fingers weave through then grip my hair as he groans. Pleasing him this way was something I always loved doing, but only with him.

"So good, Emmy," he hisses, and it only encourages me to take him deeper until the very edge of my own reflex. "Fuck, like that."

I continue my quest to make him come in my mouth by picking up my pace, the whole time watching his face with his eyes sinking back. Relaxed is what I want him to feel.

I don't stop, and my mouth moves through a motivated mission.

"You are so fucking hot right now. I can't wait to see your swollen lips as I take you deep."

Wes in bed speaks with edge, determination, and he is dominant. It turns me on, and I love it. It only makes me pick up my pace for the next minute, my mouth getting wetter around him from excitement.

Until he grips my hair and tries to pull me off him. "You're going to make me… but first I need to fuck you."

The sound of my lips sucking then popping off his cock fills the air. "But I want to fuck you." I sulk as I crawl on top of him with a playful look as he comes to sitting. I move the fabric of my panties to the side then align him with my entrance before sinking over him.

We both moan together as he slides deep inside of me, his hand bracing my hips so he can guide me through our rhythm. Every pump hits that spot inside me that makes my body sing.

Our eyes never part, and I think that is what sends the

most heat through me. It makes me nervous but equally feels right.

I love that I'm riding him, making him feel good. I love doing this with him. And I would be lying to myself if I tried to deny that I just love being with him.

Leaning forward, I continue to move on top of him with my breasts bouncing ever so slightly.

"Is this relaxing you?" I murmur into his ear as his hands move to grip my ass.

"Yes," he confirms with heavy breathing then kisses my hair.

We move slow then speed up. Our eyes continuously stay connected. This should be fun, but something right now feels like he's tying me to him with no release in sight. It doesn't scare me either.

The corner of his mouth twisting up tells me he has ideas.

"Take the lace off then get on your hands and knees," he demands, and I quickly do as he requests, moving off, throwing the damp fabric to the side, and finally kicking my heels off.

The moment that I'm on my hands and knees, Wes re-enters me and slides an arm underneath me, across my chest to pull me close to him. My ass stays in the air, but my upper body is now closer to the mattress, his breath against the skin of my cheek.

"You look perfect in every position," he mutters against my skin.

My moan is loud, as this new position means he hits me at the perfect angle.

"We'll come like this," he tells me as the fingers of his other hand comes to play with me.

The heat of his skin against mine as we move as one feels like fire.

"Fuck, Wes. I should be relaxing you, not getting fucked as deeply as humanly possible," I manage to say.

"You're relaxing me. Your perfect hot and wet pussy around my cock is heaven. Me making you come the way I want is just as good too," he tells me as he moves more vigorously. "Coming together is, however, the best."

My body jolts with electricity at every pump, my skin erupting with sweat. Yet still, he kisses my shoulder and then urges me to glance back at him. I do, and I'm met with a long passionate kiss as we both race to the finish line.

Wes moves faster and his finger doesn't stop until he stills and jerks inside of me at the moment my body begins to shudder and shake around him. An intense explosion happens between us but the sounds of the room go calm.

He kisses my back as he pulls me even closer until my little quakes ease. Only then do we both collapse. We move tactfully and slowly, so he doesn't slip out, before his leg props over my own. We both try to catch our breath as we lie there in an embrace with him still inside me.

"So, we've established that we are kind of dirty together," I drowsily mention.

His nose nuzzles into my neck and simultaneously interlinks our fingers resting between us. "Baby, we haven't even gotten to the good stuff yet."

———

WES WIPES the warm wet cloth between my legs to clean up the mark he left in me. Our eyes hold as his hand moves slowly. Then he kisses me as he throws the washcloth to the other side of the room before bringing the duvet over us. Wrapping his arms around me, I lean against his chest. This whole scene is better than my dreams. It's real.

"Feeling better?" I ask as he kisses my forehead.

"I was never not feeling good."

I smile at his stubbornness. "Come on, Wes, you were a little on edge tonight."

"Story of my life."

"I still don't get it. You and your parents have an odd relationship, yet in a non-verbal way support one another," I reflect my observation as my fingers draw lines on his chest.

"And that," his pointer finger pats the tip of my nose, "is exactly how it will forever be."

"All because they disapprove of you having a successful business, a beautiful place to live, and smart investments? I doubt that."

His eyes narrow in on me and he seems to contemplate what to say. "Now that we're sleeping together, is your loyalty with me or my sister?"

I'm thrown slightly by his question. "That's, well... how do I answer?"

"How come you never told Sadie about what happened?"

My nose scrunches as I briefly recall a conversation. "She actually asked me recently if something had ever happened between us. I felt kind of bad not being truthful, but I just didn't know what to say."

"What do you mean?"

I look at him with the same skeptical look he just flashed me. "You haven't exactly told Sadie that you and her best friend have entangled a time or two. Why?"

"That's easy. Sadie and I are not super close, but when she needs something, I am 100% there. I also don't really care about her opinion, as it wouldn't change my mind about what I want. Plus, it never crossed my mind to tell her since we were never anything yet."

"Yet?" My eyes grow large.

He chuckles under his breath as he dives in for a deep kiss on my mouth to shut me up and prove a point. Pulling away, his thumb taps my lip. "Don't pretend. You and I have always been on your mind. We just danced around one another. Now back to my original question. Is your allegiance with me or Sadie?"

"Well, I mean, there are things she tells me that I don't tell you, and I won't tell her what we talk about, which is easy, as I don't particularly want to talk to Sadie about how her brother fucks me into space."

He's amused by my comment. "Okay. I'm going to tell you something that Sadie doesn't know."

I nod instantly without a doubt, but Wes and I have kept secrets before, us being one.

"My parents are in an open marriage. I'm the lucky one who figured it out. So, when they want to judge me for my choices then they are a bit hypocritical."

My jaw hangs open at this news. Never in a million years would I have guessed this. Not John and Clarissa Bay, the parents who always welcomed me into their home and family with open arms. The couple who accompanies one another to galas and work functions like the perfect married couple of thirty-plus years.

"Okay… so that's news," I confirm.

"Sadie has no clue. I'm not sure we can really call it an open marriage since they're pretty secretive about it. It's more my dad sleeps with his much-younger secretary and my mom with an old high school boyfriend who lives a few towns away," Wes explains so casually.

"Wow. And how did you find out?" I stroke his shoulder with my hand.

He begins to laugh under his breath to himself. "*So,* I was at a guys' weekend up in Wisconsin near Lake Geneva. We had rented a house and were just going to BBQ, drink, and play some card games. I went into town to grab some extra charcoal for the grill, and as I was crossing the street, I saw dear old dad with his secretary. They didn't see me."

I do a double take. "This is crazy. So you didn't say anything?"

"Nope. Not until a few months later."

Adjusting myself slightly, I lean more on my side to watch his facial expressions.

"We had a little confrontation a few months ago," he tells me but doesn't look at me.

"You mean a debate?"

"Sure. We said a lot of things. I threw the poker story at him to piss him off—bad move on my part. Anyhow, he explained the arrangement he and my mom have."

I quickly kiss his cheek. "Okay, but I guess it is their prerogative how they want to run their marriage."

"True, just a little surprising."

"I guess your relationship just changed a little."

"We… had that *debate* a few days before his heart attack." Wes's eyes turn to me to ensure I grasp the timeline.

My hand reaches out to caress his cheek. I want to wrap my arms around him and cradle him, but our bodies are already entwined.

"It's not your fault," I assure him.

A devilish grin forms on his mouth. "No, it isn't. It's Tracy's, the secretary who was giving my dad a blowjob at the time."

When his sentence sinks in and I realize that he isn't joking, we both erupt in laughter.

In our hysteria, he pulls and squeezes me closer. Something tells me that Wes is going to be just fine.

"See, you relaxed me so much that we can joke about this. Only you have that magical ability with me."

Only me.

That hits my heart and sends excitement through me, because I've always wanted it to be only me.

EMILY

"This is where you belong." His gravelly morning voice speaks into my ear, his arms wrapping around me from behind while I cook eggs. "You have no idea how many times I've wanted to see you in my college shirt and nothing else but a ridiculous excuse for panties." His fingers playfully snap the waistband of my thong that I had in my purse, because—yeah—I may have changed the contents of my bag recently, *just in case.*

I do my best to shake him off me, as I have an unguarded smile on my face. "Me and half of the female population," I retort back.

He backs away, pretending to be offended, and he puts his hands in the air. "Whoa, whoa, whoa. Don't make me bend you over and show you how wrong you are."

"Maybe that's what I want." I flash him a sexy look, complete with the spatula gesturing toward him, before turning to dish up the eggs.

We each take a plate, and although we could go sit at his dining table or kitchen island, we both hop on opposite counters and ravish our plates, as we're starving—understandably.

"I need to check in at Jupiter and make sure Charlie and I are good, but after, do you want to head to Navy Pier for a walk then grab dinner?" Wes asks casually as he moves some eggs on his plate.

Slowly I swallow my eggs and decide to correct him. "We're having fun, not dating."

The sound of the fork dropping to his plate startles me, and in a flash, he sets his plate down before hopping off the counter and coming to me, with his talented hands resting on each side of me.

"We're back to this? Last night was 100% your initiation," he reminds me, and his head and eyes tilt up to try and capture my gaze.

"It was, *but…* we can just have fun, right? Distract one another when the other needs it?"

"Emmy." His tone warns me as his finger hooks under my jaw to hold my head in place so I can only look at him. Wes steps between my knees, urging my thighs to open. Heat is already coiling inside me.

"Let's be honest for a second. Can I only be just fun to you?" he asks, and I do my best to stay silent, but his eyes show me he will wait for an answer.

"You aren't just fun to me," Wes informs me, and I love that he's laying it all out. "So, tell me truthfully what you believe. The guy you're falling for and the guy who is right there with you on that."

My head perks up when he says that, and I feel my cheekbones tighten. "Wes." My words get stuck as everything inside me dances, and I just want to kiss him.

"Tell me," he reminds me he is waiting on an answer.

"You're right… you will always be more to me."

He leans down to seal our lips together.

"Good, we're aligned," He speaks against my lips before crashing our mouths into another kiss.

I fist the fabric of his t-shirt at his chest to encourage him to break our kiss. "I just don't know what this means," I admit. "It's kind of complicated."

He caresses my cheek tenderly as his eyes blaze with warmth.

"No, it's not. So let me take you on a date. The kind that you so desperately want to tell Sadie about but won't because it's me."

Ahh, his captivating grin is out in full force today.

"A date would mean people may see us together, with you as more than just my boss," I highlight this fact.

He leans in to kiss my neck. "Absolutely, since I can't keep my hands off of you."

I have to push him away slightly. "What about this? We can continue to see each other, but privately?"

"Are we continuing to see each other in a romantic capacity or a fun capacity?" he asks, double-checking he understands.

I debate for a second. "Can we not label it right now? Just go with the flow?"

He studies me for a second, but then quickly smiles. "Sure, we can go with the flow."

It makes me nervous that he just agreed so easily. There must be a loophole I missed somewhere. However, I can't think about that now as Wes bends his knees to lean down and begins to trail kisses up my bare thigh.

"What are you doing?" I give him a curious look.

He glances up at me. "Showing you that I am in agreement."

"But you already said… oh, fuck." His fingers glide over

the fabric of my panties, before hooking under then circulating my clit, and I should be embarrassed his fingers are instantly coated in my arousal.

"You're ready." His eyes peer up at me with a look of approval. "Has our entire conversation gotten you excited?" he asks as he pulls my panties down and off.

"I'm not answering, as everything I say only encourages you." My voice is already raspy.

Wes pulls me to the edge of the counter in a swift move and he lowers his boxer briefs just enough before sliding into me and making me yelp in pure pleasure.

"You only have to look at me and you encourage me. Now I'm going to show you how much." He breathes near my ear as he thrusts with purpose in and out of me.

"Wes," I cry out, as I'm barely hanging on.

"Tell me you were ready for me, because I'm yours."

I'm so overwhelmed from the stretch around him and his cock hitting all my nerves inside me. It feels like bliss.

"You're mine." My voice is hoarse and answers without thought as I grip his muscly arms tighter.

"Exactly, and you're mine. Tell me."

"I'm yours." I'm on the brink, my voice ragged.

He thrusts so deep that I'm not sure I've ever discovered this angle.

My arms loop around his neck and my fingers claw the fabric of his shirt as our mouths meld together.

He takes me there on his kitchen counter, and it's only when I am nearly panting his name that I realize the man already threw the loophole at me. He got me to admit to more, and it only makes me smile.

———

"THIS IS TOTALLY INAPPROPRIATE," I tell Wes as I stand in the middle of his office waving the small bag he just handed to me. My glare is full of disapproval, but good God, I'm struggling not to smile.

"Hey, I closed the door, so we are in private and I'm respecting your rules. Going with the flow," he answers me as he sits perched on the end of his desk, looking like an image of pure smolder.

Glancing into the bag once more, I can't do it. My smirk can't be contained any longer.

It's been a few days since our conversation in his kitchen. In that time, I've learned that, for a man who owns a restaurant, he is horrible at cooking; even jarred pasta sauce can't be saved. Wes also enjoys listening to podcasts about the stock market and can still do a hundred push-ups... unless I'm lying under him—he gets sidetracked.

He also gets me.

As proven by the bag hanging off my finger that is carefully wrapped with pink tissue paper and handed to me a few moments ago by the devil himself.

"Points for originality," I compliment as I close the bag filled with a pair of dark purple satin panties and a few stacks of purple post-it notes.

Stepping to Wes, he reaches forward to encircle his arms around me then pulls me flush until we're joined at the middle.

"I thought we could shake up that planning wall of yours with a new color."

"Oh? How so?" I'm curious as I straighten the collar of his shirt.

"Well, I figured out each color is for a certain subject. As much as purple isn't my color, I think you definitely need a color for our planning, and the other colors were taken." He leans in to kiss the corner of my mouth.

"I could *maybe* be on board with that. What do you have in mind?"

"How about we start with a date outside the walls of our apartments? Before you even say it, trust me."

My head retreats back a few inches and my lips part. Gosh, his eyes connect with my heart and make it so easy for me to agree.

"Okay."

"Good. It's a surprise, so how about we meet two blocks away later to grab a cab on the corner?" he suggests.

My face must be glowing. I love his efforts to respect my wishes, and I love surprises.

"Sounds like you're scheming… but I am on board," I confirm and kiss him quickly.

I TAP the paper on the bar top that lists the timetable for the opening event. "I would definitely increase the time for welcome drinks by fifteen minutes. People always arrive late or get wrapped up in conversation."

"That makes sense," Charlie replies then scribbles a note on the paper where he's sitting next to me.

The ping from my phone makes me look at my notifications and I see an e-mail pop up. Briefly I glance at it, as Charlie seems lost in thought anyhow.

Reading the e-mail, I'm surprised. It's one of the more senior managers from the old company that I worked for. She's asking if I would be interested in meeting up about a position at the company she's now starting of specialty cocktails in a bottle.

A sound escapes me, and Charlie looks at me with piqued interest.

"Everything okay?"

"Yeah," I sigh. "A little strange, that's all. Someone from my old company is starting a new business and wants to discuss a job. As much as a woman-owned business is appealing, it also isn't, as I have no interest in Boston or corporate events. Just funny to get these e-mails. It's sort of a reminder, you know?"

"Can't say I have that problem but makes sense what you say. Anyhow, I don't think I have any further questions now, and the clock tells me I need to head home too. Doing anything special tonight?" he asks as he hops off the stool and grabs his phone that was lying on the bar top.

"Oh, uh, plans? No. Not really," I lie and somehow manage to sound normal. Inside, I'm so excited and have been glancing at the time non-stop for the last hour. I think internally somewhere, my body started counting the seconds too.

"Okay, well, have a relaxing night in," he says with a soft smile.

"You too."

I watch him walk away back to the kitchen down the hall. The moment that he is out of my vision, I scan the room, and with no one noticing me, I grab my bag that I already brought down and the sweater I kept on the back of the chair.

On my way out, I quickly glance into my compact and fluff my hair. When that's done, I apply a new layer of lip gloss to my lips. With haste, I walk the two blocks, and the moment I turn the corner and see Wes standing there my heart melts.

I saw him earlier today in his jeans, blazer, and light blue button-down, but it is oh-so better when I get down the block and see him waiting for me.

My smile spreads as I make the last few steps closer to him. We stand close enough with giddy smiles as we wait for the cab.

"Ready?" he asks.

"Depends. Is this where you tell me you're a member of some secret sex club?" I sarcastically ask.

Lines form on his forehead. "Remind me again to figure out all your kinks," he says as the cab pulls up to the curb.

He opens the door, and we get in. Once we're settled, we look at one another then meet for a welcoming kiss that's all parts warm and fuzzy.

"So, that surprise," he tells me with a look of pure magic in his eyes as his thumb rubs along my cheek. "Remember that summer when we would look at the stars from the back of my car?"

My hand rests on his thigh. "You thought I would forget?"

"No, but I do think we should repeat it."

"As in here? The back of this cab?" I'm beginning to wonder about his plan.

"You're cute sometimes. Not here, but I am taking you to see the stars."

It's still too early in the evening for dark skies, but Wes looks so proud of what he has planned that I don't dare question it.

Instead, I tell him what is honestly the truth. "You know, I always dreamed about Romantic Wes, but he is so much better in real life."

The man actually blushes a little then kisses my cheek before interlacing our hands to rest on his thigh.

It is a comforting few minutes more of an elated blissful

silence in the car. It's only when I figure out our direction that I realize he is true to his word, and something inside me stirs, hoping this is the first of many nights ahead.

WES

"What are you laughing about?" I only reminded her that I asked if she wanted to go to the gift shop and she started giggling. Then she turned hysterical when I showed her the space rocks they were trying to sell.

"It's nothing, I promise. You'll see," she replies, touching my arm.

I have no clue what is going on. "Okay, so that's a no to the giftshop after the show. Are you sure this isn't cheesy?" I ask Emily as I hold her hand and we sit in our recliner chairs inside the planetarium.

The perfect spot for a date. Tonight, it's over twenty-one only, so we don't have to worry about kids running around. It's also a dimly lit place, which also gets bonus points. How I managed to come up with this idea surprises even me.

She brings my hand to her lips to kiss. "Are you kidding me? I love it."

It was pure coincidence they have a show about Jupiter happening. It's not that busy, and even while we wait, the mood of the place is set. It's romantic. 100% romantic.

"The last time I was here was in sixth grade for a field

trip," she says. "I like who I'm sitting next to this time so much more."

"Oh yeah? Who were you stuck with in the sixth grade?" I ask.

"Don't remember his name, but he definitely had food stuck in his braces." She glances at me before looking around the room in wonder.

"I guess it's an easy step up then," I note.

Resting her head on my shoulder, she squeezes my arm and lets out a sigh. "It's kind of funny that here we are, you and me."

"You mean that this thing between us started back in college? I'm not sure it was our time then. I wish it were, but we were in two totally different places."

"Trust me, I wish it went differently too. But I get it and can agree there is no way it would have worked."

I kiss the top of her head and inhale the scent of her hair, which only makes the corners of my mouth curve—she smells of my shampoo.

"Last year, on the other hand…" Her tone is almost playful. "I'm not sure I made the right decision; it would have been fun."

"Then what?" I ask.

"No clue. I guess… our timing ended up the way it was supposed to." She looks up at me, and even in the dim light, her face almost has an enchanted glow.

Another obvious fact dawns on me that we never mentioned. "I should have called you."

"You mean last year?"

"Yeah, explain everything or say I wanted to fly out to see you."

"Then what, Wes? Long-distance wasn't for either of us… and I could have texted you or called."

"When?"

She gives me a wicked smirk. "When I was lying in your bed alone."

I have to shake my head and groan at the reminder before I tickle her side. "Stop reminding me of what I missed."

"Okay, okay."

I re-angle slightly to ensure my body faces her. "We were always going to circle back to each other, and you know that too."

She gently shakes her head. "I didn't always know."

Her words disappoint me and scare me that the scale is slightly one-sided between us.

And then her words instantly bring relief to me. "I always hoped it."

Right on cue, the room darkens and the noise of the small crowd hushes, but I quickly lean in to steal a kiss from Emmy, and she's making me crazy the way she adds her tongue. We both struggle to pull apart.

During the whole show, our hands cling to one another, and we steal glances. I couldn't care less what the narrator of the show says about stardust and galaxies bursting. I have Emmy right here next to me. And I don't care if the night goes black if it means I can have her forever—plus, her eyes alone are two little moons.

Every time her eyes meet mine, I wonder if the same timeframe crosses her mind too. Forever.

SHE HASN'T STOPPED BITING her bottom lip or grinning since we got back to my place, and I set us up in the middle of my living room on the floor. "You are just full of surprises today." Her tone is playful and she crawls to me on her hands and knees to kiss my mouth.

How the hell am I supposed to keep this a romantic dinner without skipping to dessert? And I'm still not sure how candles ended up in my place. My guess is Sadie left them when she lived here last summer. Either way, they are getting good use now, fully lit and scattered around the room, with music softly on in the background.

My A-game romance ideas today mean we have now ended up with a romantic picnic in my living room. Never have I constantly wanted to surprise someone and always put my best foot forward. I've become a sappy man.

"Finish your dinner. You need energy for later." I indicate with my chopstick to her takeout box of Thai food.

"Sure thing, boss." She winks at me before returning to sitting on her knees then biting into her food. "Are you ready for the big day? It's coming up real soon."

"I am. I kind of feel like I've been looking forward to it for so long that I just want it to be over with already. It's time," I say, before throwing the remnants of my spring roll onto the plate and grabbing my beer bottle.

"I can imagine, and you should be so excited. The place is ready. I can't wait to recommend Jupiter to clients—when I actually have clients." She sets her box down and grabs her wine to drink. "I almost forgot to tell you, I filed for my LLC so should get that all squared away in ten-to-fifteen business days. I didn't think of a creative name so just registered under my own. Boring, I know, but maybe Layla can help me with a logo and website. It's kind of real now."

"That's amazing. See, you ripped that band-aid off. Guess that means you have more room on your post-it wall for my notes." I raise a brow at her.

"They're going to be dirty, aren't they?"

"Some of them, yeah." I take a sip of my beer. "Now what's next on your list?" I scoot closer to her because I can never get enough of touching her, even if it's an innocent side hug. Or listening to her plans, even when they don't always involve me.

"Start to think about potential clients to approach, and I'll definitely need to really look at the finance part again."

"Say the word and I can have a look," I remind her as I set my bottle to the side.

Her hand squeezes my thigh from appreciation, but it opens that energy channel that goes straight to my dick.

"Just need to brush up my portfolio a little, and hopefully my current boss will give me a good recommendation."

"I think you can persuade him," I warn her with a wink.

"You'll still see me when I'm no longer working for you —and without restrictions too," she jokes and gives me side-eye.

"Don't tempt me right now." My head moves side to side.

"To do what?" She places her glass down.

I grab her wrist to pull her to my direction. "Spank you."

Her eyes blaze a look that I can only describe as a cross between surprise and curiosity. It completely turns me on, and then something vibrates between us that makes her laugh. It's my phone in my pocket.

I quickly pull it out. "Let me turn it off." I quickly glance at it. "Hold on."

LOGAN

Alright, time to meet up.

COLE

Oh, are you finally back from the honeymoon phase and ready to settle into life as a man who will forever be wrong and his wife always right?

LOGAN

Geez, clearly the past few weeks haven't changed you. Did I miss anything else?

COLE

Why don't you ask Wes. He's been too busy to meet up with me.

A slew of emojis floods the next message. Winks, smiley faces with crowns, eggplants, tigers, and it goes on.

LOGAN

Did someone hook up with the maid of honor? My money is on that. I mean, I guess I can keep bro code for this.

COLE

...until your wife holds you down and threatens you with no sex. Then I know you will desert us in a heartbeat.

LOGAN

True. I do like it when she tries to hold me down.

Quickly I type with my thumb.

ME

Hey, fuckers, that's my sister you're talking about.

I throw in a waving emoji.

Me

Can we re-think our topic choices in this group chat?

LOGAN

Absolutely right, man. So there is news?

I have to grin at this conversation until Emily nudges my arm.

"Everything okay there?" She tries to look at my phone.

I grunt a laugh. "Yeah, sure. My brother-in-law and his best friend can just be a bit much sometimes."

"Guess that means Sadie and Logan are out of their bubble?" Her brows raise.

I nod yes.

"I'll talk to her at some point, or maybe we should do it together. Shit. Ruby." She curses to herself and rubs her forehead. "Totally forgot to call her back, I was so wrapped up in my stuff. I think something happened at the wedding."

A low rumbling chuckle escapes me, and I hold a finger up for her to wait. Quickly I type on my phone as Emmy moves to clear away the dishes.

ME

New topic. By any chance did Cole get up to something or someone at the wedding?

COLE

Not cool, man.

LOGAN

Fuck, what did my wedding do to you people?

ME

Nothing new to me. Anyhow, I'm offline for a while. Busy night.

And because I need to shout it out to someone.

ME

...with a particular woman.

I decide to live on the edge, and I add a winking emoji

before turning my phone to silent, and I toss my phone onto the couch.

Looking at Emily and I see a lazy smile on her face as she returns from the kitchen with her eyes staring at me. She's up to something. "Want to play strip Go Fish?" she asks as she tosses me a deck of cards, and it makes me laugh.

"You mean strip poker?"

"Uhm, no. I don't know how to play poker, and something tells me that would take too long anyhow. Plus, you would win." Her voice is sultry and smooth like silk.

"Go Fish it is then." I grin and quickly open the deck of cards.

The whole time that I shuffle the cards, we are in a face-off, and her tongue rolls along her teeth to the corner of her mouth, which is kind of torturous. I don't even look at the cards as I deal them out.

"Ladies first," I say.

She bats her lashes and I swear purposely tilts her body forward so her cleavage taunts me when she looks at her cards.

"Have any twos?"

"Go fish."

Her smirk forms as she slowly punishes me and peels her sweater top off to leave her in a black bra and jeans.

"Have any eights?" I ask with a raised brow.

"Go fish."

I reply by quickly getting my shirt off.

This goes on until I'm in my boxers and she is popping the button of her jeans. The moment her jeans move down a few inches and I see that she's wearing the dark purple satin that I got her, I'm a dead man. She just slayed me, and the whole night she has been wearing them, which in turn makes my balls heavy with want for her.

"You know I had a two." I'm smug and totally lying, but I want to tease her.

Her jaw drops low as she kicks her jeans off. "You cheated?"

I challenge her as I throw my cards in the air. "What are you going to do about it?"

She is on her hands and knees again in a flash, crawling to me, and the heat ignited between us is a fucking wildfire now. Moving on top of me to straddle, she circles her hips to rub herself on me, and energy runs through my veins. Without thought, the palm of my hand lands on her pert ass for a step up from playful to a quite firm spank.

Her eyes blaze into wide saucers as her mouth opens before a look of excitement floods her face. "I should definitely punish you," she murmurs as her mouth kisses the base of my throat.

"Make me go down on you," I beg as my fingers dig into the flesh of her behind, causing her to grind on top of me.

Her finger hushes my mouth. "Nuh-uh. I want to go down on you."

"Then we both go down on each other." I give her knowing eyes, and it makes her hum in satisfaction.

Her thumb rubs my lips. "I had a really good night," she says sincerely and pausing us in this moment.

"Me too. We should have had one of these nights long ago."

A faint smile appears on her. "We have it now."

I move to encourage her mouth to meet me halfway for a long kiss. The kind where she drives me insane because she playfully pulls away then traces my lips barely with her own. Her hand firmly grips my cock.

"Slow. I want to go slow with you tonight," I softly inform her, and I feel her smile against the skin of my neck.

"I want that too," she mumbles.

Then we're back at it.

I encourage her to lie on her side with her head angled toward my cock, and I lie on my side with my head diving between her thighs. All right there on my living room floor.

At the same time our mouths descend on the other, landing exactly where we both want.

18

EMILY

Watching Wes do push-ups in the middle of his living room is the perfect way to start my day. And it's been this way a few mornings this week. Since our date, it feels like it's the rhythm we were always meant to have—mornings together after sleeping blissfully in each other's arms all night.

Walking to him, wearing his button-down shirt and nothing else except a coffee mug in hand, I smile to myself as I move to interrupt him.

"Sixty-one, sixty-two…" he counts as he focuses on his push-ups.

Setting the mug on the floor, I bend down then slide underneath his arms to quickly lie under him.

"By all means, keep counting," I say with a look that I know is very sultry.

He gives me a grimace as he continues. "You are the perfect motivation."

"Am I now?"

He moves down and pecks my mouth with a kiss before pushing back up.

"I'm getting slightly sidetracked now, though," he warns as he slows his movement then nestles his nose into my neck.

"Oh gee, surely that's not me." I play dumb and wrap my legs around his middle as he grazes my skin with his teeth and collapses on top of me.

"Emmy," he growls.

I laugh, scurry off him, and reach for the mug of coffee. "Here, I brought you coffee."

We both adjust to sitting up as I hand him the cup. "*Coffee* coffee or your healthy crap?" he double-checks, because somewhere in the last week, he surprised me with keeping a jar of chicory coffee at his place so I have the option.

"Relax, real coffee. I know you need everything perfect today," I assure him, and his eyes study me and that glint in his eye draws me in. "What are you thinking?"

His arm reaches out to invite me closer and I slide to him so his arms wrap around me, and he sits behind me.

"This time tomorrow, I can check Jupiter off my list," he mentions, and I admire how relaxed he is considering tonight is his big night. "Then I can focus on my next project."

"Already?"

"Yeah, why not? Maybe I should see what the reviews say first, but I can look into taking on a few more silent investments or even finding another apartment then rent that out as a real estate investment. Options are endless."

I glance behind me to peer up to his face. "You really have big plans." I'm in awe that he's calm and thinking of his future, as if tonight is a tiny speck in his life.

"And tonight is a big night for you too. Just you watch, everyone will love your work."

I snort a laugh. "You haven't even seen what I've done yet, boss."

"I said you could have free rein, and I meant it." He gently kisses my forehead.

"It also means after tonight that you are no longer my boss—"

"Nuh-uh." His sweltering look is filled with confidence. "Sure, in work. But I think we both know I will still boss you around in other areas of our life."

I like how he says *our life*, but I don't dissect his sentence too much because I know what he's indicating. "You mean in the bedroom?"

"You are such a smart cookie." He kisses the corner of my mouth, to which I respond by capturing his mouth with my own with the faint taste of coffee on his lips.

Pulling away, his thumb strokes my cheek the way I always like it. "Tonight could open a lot of doors for you and also for me."

"Hopefully. I'd really like to get everything moving with my freelance stuff, and then maybe in a year, be stable enough for a nice long vacay."

"Right, Victoria Island." He grins, as it means he has been snooping around in my notebook. I don't really mind, either. I've found a little note the other day literally listing Wes as an option for the main menu of a small function Jupiter was having.

Playfully I hit him. "On that note, I should get ready for work. I would hate to be late, my boss has a thing for punishment." I smirk as I stand up and offer my hand to Wes.

He joins me in standing. "I wish I could show you what kind of punishment I would have in mind, but I need to run an errand before heading to Jupiter."

"Really? Today is the day you have last-minute errands? Shall I go do it for you? You really need to be at Jupiter for

Charlie. There's so much to do before all the guests arrive," I remind him as we walk toward his bedroom.

"Trust me, it's fine. You've already showered?" he asks as he begins to undress.

"Yeah, I'll change then head out, because I really want to start by nine with setting up," I mention as I grab my clothes from my bag on the chair.

"Okay, I'll be quick."

I give him an assuring glance then get to work on getting dressed, smiling to myself like a giddy girl. The other day I picked out a new black dress. I wanted something stunning, yet simple for tonight. Even though I'm not there as Wes's other half, I know his eyes will land on me a few times. Is it crazy that I want him to think I look like the complete package?

Looking through my purse for my makeup, I freeze when I see my birth control pack. Why does it feel like I haven't seen them in a while? Surveying the room, I hear the running of water in the shower and know Wes is in there. Quickly opening the pack, I look and realize that I definitely forgot one yesterday. My fingers frantically count the rest and, yep, forgot one or two the other week too. In fact, it seems this whole month I have failed at this. What the fuck? I never forget them. Ever.

Recalling the last five minutes of conversation and all the plans Wes and I have career wise, I know I can say with confidence that this screw-up is nowhere on our agenda. But I can't think too much into it. I have so much to do today, and Wes needs to focus. This has to wait until tomorrow, and it could mean absolutely nothing too.

Sighing, I throw the pack back in to my bag and brush the situation to the back of my head. This is no big deal. It can't be.

"Everything okay?" Wes asks as he walks back into the room with a towel wrapped around his waist. "You seem a little spaced out."

"Totally fine. Just excited for today," I lie as he gently kisses the round edge of my shoulder.

"Me too."

Looking at him, I feel like everything will be perfectly alright. That's the only way it can go tonight.

19

WES

"Are you ready?" Emily whispers into my ear, and I can feel her leaning up on her tippy toes as she tries to cover my eyes with her hands.

The opening is in a few hours, and everything is all set up, but I wasn't allowed to look until she and Charlie said so.

"More than ever," I reply, and I'm already squinting my eyes from anticipation.

"It's all yours, this place," she reminds me before removing her hands.

My eyes blink a few times to adjust to the restaurant. It looks spectacular. Emily added extra white fairy lights everywhere, dimmed the normal lighting, and there are tall dark blue candles lit on every table. I'm speechless as I step closer to a made-up table set perfectly with white china and dark napkins. Then there are touches of gold and silver in little places such as the centerpieces and the small gift bags tied with ribbon set on every plate.

"Look in the bag," she encourages as her hands clasp together, and when I glance to her, I see she's excited to watch me open it.

My eyes tilt up to her with an approving look as I open the small bag, and as soon as I pull out the contents, I am in awe.

"I thought the guests could leave with a mix. So, we have little bottles of olive oil from the farm, which is the oil we use to serve with the bread. Small pack of mints with the Jupiter logo on it. A chocolate truffle, and well… a space rock."

Quickly my head turns to her, and our eyes meet. Her mouth is struggling to decide whether to smile or not. Pulling the palm-sized rock up to the light, it almost glitters, and it has the name and opening date on it. It's elegant and perfect to be placed on a desk.

"Where did you find this?" I wonder, as it never in a million years would have crossed my mind.

She steps closer to me, but only just as she scans the room. "I… I contacted the planetarium a few weeks ago. Spoke to someone in the gift shop."

My own heart is about to outshine this damn rock in my hand. "So, you had already been to the gift shop?" I now connect the dots.

"Yep." Her head bobs. "It's not a rock from Jupiter or an actual space rock, but it's the idea. I thought by adding an engraving in gold that it would be elegant enough. If you don't like it then we don't have to inclu—"

My eyes pierce her own. "No way. I love it, and I wish more than anything you would let me kiss you right now."

"It's good you don't because Charlie is walking this way," she tells me without blinking.

"Emily knocked it out of the park, right?" Charlie asks, oblivious to the fact that I'm getting serenaded by Emmy simply through our eyes firmly set on each other.

"She did amazing," I say and look at Charlie.

"Well, I will let Charlie fill you in on the rest," Emily

mentions as she glances to the floor between Charlie and me. "I think the marketing guys are arriving soon and wanted to double-check where to set up for photos."

"Oh yeah, press wants a piece of Wes. Are they still interviewing you for that feature, successful bachelors under thirty?" Charlie sounds clearly entertained.

"What?" Emily chokes out a laugh. "No way. Is that really a thing?" Now she's interested in the news.

"It is *not* a bachelor feature. They are coming for the restaurant, and Josh mentioned *maybe* they want to include me on some ridiculous list," I try to clarify the situation to everyone.

"Sure. Well, they're here in half an hour." Emily looks at her schedule on a paper.

"And I need ten minutes for you to double-check your wine options with the bar staff," Charlie asks me.

"No problem," I answer to him then try to grab Emily's attention who is busy looking at her pages of notes. "Emily, can we meet once more before you speak with Josh and Noah?"

She searches between Charlie and me for a clue and reluctantly begins to answer, "Sure. Let me go change for tonight first."

———

"WHAT IS SO URGENT? Everything okay? Did I miss something that we need for tonight?" she asks as she stalks toward me, looking concerned.

A satisfied look plays on my mouth as I sit at the edge of my desk and survey her in the black form-fitting dress she threw on and is already making my head spin. "Relax. Everything looks exceptional. You really did exactly what I needed someone to do, and I'm still a little speechless for everything downstairs. And those space rocks will be a story for us one day. Now come here." My hands reach out to grab her hanging hand then tug her closer to me. "But I'm not sure how long the marketing stuff is going to be or how busy tonight will get. Or if we will be too tired later tonight…" I prompt her.

"Oh. I mean, it's a crazy night, I just assumed you would want to head home to sleep." She seems to be busy in double-checking her list. "Seems like you have everything you need for the next few hours."

A long silence fills the room and I decide this is my moment.

"I almost have everything on hand for tonight, but there is one thing missing," I begin, and my hand sneaks into my inner blazer pocket. "Come closer," I invite her, and I love how she obeys and steps closer until we're touching by the edges of our clothing.

"What's missing?" she innocently asks.

"You."

It makes her lick her lips and her cheeks to squeeze before her grin displays on her face and pink floods her skin. Then I make her face turn to surprise when she sees that I have a blue Tiffany's box in my hand. Bigger than a ring box, but small enough that she knows it's jewelry.

"It's completely inappropriate for my boss to be holding that in front of me." Her tone is neutral, and I can see she's trying to hold it together.

"It's also completely inappropriate what your dress is doing to me or the thoughts it's imprinting in my head too, but I'll let it go."

Opening the box, I show her the bracelet that looks like a chain with a lock and has a few pearls on it.

"I want you by my side tonight." I grab the bracelet from the box and throw the box to the side.

"I will be there and will make sure everything is perfect," she reassures me and is still looking at my hands in slight shock.

"No, I mean as my girlfriend. The one who supports me, and I support her. I want everyone to know that you are mine," I explain as I grab her wrist to clasp the bracelet on.

I'm done playing games. Tonight is one of the biggest nights of my life career-wise, and I want her here as the woman I can show off as my own and make it clear to everyone that she is my future.

I lean in to steal a kiss, but she moves to avoid me. "Wes, I …" She quickly steps away and nervously nibbles her lip. "I want that too, but if I have any hope of starting out my new business right, then it still stands what I have always said. It doesn't help me if people think I got this job because I'm with you."

Oh yeah, *that* factor.

"I promise after the dust settles on all of the hype this place is going to get then we will get there. I just need a little time."

Stepping to her, I grab both of her arms so she can't escape me. "Emmy, you have more confidence than you let yourself believe. Have you ever considered that you've knocked this event so out of the park that nobody will even notice if I kiss you after thanking everyone in my welcome speech? They won't care because your talent is more distracting."

"It's not a confidence thing, it's a sound decision," she tries to debate me.

"That's bullshit."

"We have so much happening in the next twelve hours,

maybe we shouldn't make it more complicated. I mean, Sadie should probably get a heads-up."

I don't like how she's making excuses.

"Do you not want this? Us, I mean?"

Her eyes snap up to mine. "I do want us, that's why I'm saying now isn't the time to announce that we've been sleeping together. It doesn't look great for you either, or fair to Charlie or Reggie who put in so many more hours than me to help Jupiter. Neither of us wants them to feel like you're playing favorites or to make them feel uncomfortable. I promise, we will be able to shout us from the rooftops one day… just not… tonight," she pleads.

Emily brings her hands to cradle my face and her thumb strokes my cheek, which already calms me down a level. "I promise, Wes. You've never left my mind since the first time you kissed me, so why would I start forgetting you now?" I see the honesty in her eyes and hear the vulnerability in her voice. "Please?"

"I don't like it, but what's waiting a little longer? But promise me something?" I pull her flush to me as she nods in agreement. "Wear the bracelet so I know you're mine."

Her lips find mine to kiss me long and hard, then she speaks against my lips as my hands roam her hips. "It's beautiful. Why did you get me this?"

"I wanted to get you something, and I know how much you love charms and chains." I give her a grimace. "I think I'll love seeing your wrist working me with this on too." I kiss the side of her neck as her palm slams softly against my chest.

"Thank you, but you shouldn't have. Was this your secret errand earlier?" She shakes her hand in the air to show the bracelet.

I nod. "I swung by the store when it opened."

"I'm never taking it off."

"Never is a long time."

"We'll talk about that another day." She winks at me before meeting me for another kiss that makes us both moan and debate if we should christen my desk quickly. Alas, I have to get to an interview, so we don't get far.

Emily stops in the doorway. "Oh yeah, don't forget to double-check the guest list. I had contact with everyone except the ones in yellow, you said you would."

I tilt my chin up in agreement. "Sure. I'll do that as I head downstairs."

She gives me a subtle grin. "Look at you, Mr. Bigshot. I always knew you would end up here." Emmy flashes her eyes before heading off.

It makes me smile to myself as I remember her faith in me, even when we were younger. I pull up my phone and look at the guest list. It's in that moment, to my slight horror, that I forgot about a little factor. No way did I do it on purpose, I've just literally been in a world that has revolved around Jupiter, Emmy, and my bed plus Emmy.

Those elements can easily make a man sidetracked.

It's not a big deal, but it's probably a decent thing to give Emmy the heads-up that one of the bloggers is not only slightly clingy, but someone I dated briefly.

20

EMILY

All eyes stare at Wes as he stands on one of the middle steps with a glass of champagne in hand, his look a stance between handsome-make-your-knees-weak and sexy-as-hell-make-your-panties-drenched.

I haven't seen Wes since a few hours ago when he made my heart want to dance and my body hum as he stood in front of me, telling me the words I've been waiting to hear my entire adult life… okay, my teenage life too.

I'm his and he is mine. We are an us.

I can't wait to shout it to everyone, and my chest has felt a thousand butterflies flying around for the last few hours. Luckily, I have been busy with last-minute touches, and everyone has wanted a piece of Wes since. Our brief few minutes in his office earlier were probably our last today, which is fine. Tonight is his night.

"Thank you all for coming. I hope you enjoy dinner tonight, a taste of all the good things to come." I melt when he looks faintly in my direction, a move only I would notice. "It's nice to be back in Chicago and be able to share this with family and friends. More importantly, if you're going to open a restaurant, then where better than the city that does food and style like no other. The ambience of this place during the day is ideal for that business lunch, and in the evenings it's the escape you want to have with your romantic date. I'm excited to finally welcome you all. Cheers." Wes tilts his glass up and the room erupts in a cheer before the music picks up again.

My eyes are glued to Wes as people swarm to him, including his father. I can't hear what they're saying, but for once the scene feels different between them. His father's hand on Wes's shoulder as he says something only Wes can hear. Then Wes looks at his father to double-check, and when neither man's face changes, then a faint smile forms on Wes's face. Any passerby could tell that his father said something profound or at least sincere. He looks like a man who is proud.

That makes me happy for Wes. He should get everything he wants.

"I can't believe my brother did all of this," Sadie says in amazement as she sips from her drink, a club soda, I think. I forgot she was standing next to me. Logan is at the bar with Cole.

"He did well, right?" I can't help answering proudly, and my cheeks are beginning to hurt from the smile that won't relent tonight.

Sadie taps my shoulder with her own. "You also played a part in tonight. Everyone will be asking for your name, I'm sure."

"Maybe. How was your honeymoon? We need to catch up. I've been so busy that I kind of ignored Ruby, so I get an award for horrible person this month," I speak as I look around the busy room.

A total mix of business professionals and millennials, but

everyone has a drink in hand and they're standing in little groups in deep conversation with laughter. The DJ in the corner plays a subtle lounge mix that isn't Wes's style, but it fits the ambiance for tonight.

"Honeymoon was heaven, and I would say we will talk about it later, but I doubt you want the rundown on what I did on my honeymoon considering we barely left the room." She smirks to herself proudly.

It makes me shoot my eyes to Sadie and shake my head slightly before I weave my fingers through my hair and blow out a breath.

"Whoa, is that new?" Sadie asks and she tilts her chin to indicate to my wrist.

Looking, I see that my new bracelet is very visible, because it is, well, a bracelet. "Oh, this? Uhm, yeah, it's new."

Sadie gives me a knowing look. "Is it now?" She studies me, and I feel like she has developed a theory about what her brother and I get up to. "A story you need to share another time?" she asks confidently before taking a sip from her tumbler.

"Sadie, I…" I want to tell her, but now isn't the time, as proven by the fact that Layla and Lauren come join us. They're here since Noah and Josh are handling the marketing for tonight. Lauren just happens to also work for Logan and is Cole's sister.

"Gorgeous place," Lauren mentions as she brushes some of her blond hair behind her shoulders.

"This for sure will be the new hotspot. It was popular before when it was Two Tomatoes, but this is next-level elegant," Layla says as she grabs an appetizer from a waiter walking by with a tray.

"Oh, I wanted to ask if you are taking clients already. I

remember you mentioned at Sadie's wedding that you were starting your own business," Lauren asks excitedly.

"She is. Why, do you need someone?" Sadie now sounds like my PR lady and the woman who gets energy from gossip.

My hand touches Sadie's shoulder to encourage her to settle down. "I am, but more private events, not really corporate stuff. Do you need help with something?"

Lauren smiles brightly and wiggles her ring finger.

"Wow! You didn't have that a few weeks ago." I smile and look at the ring she shows me on her finger. It's not small, that's for sure.

"It's new, but I am not a wedding-planner type of person, and then Layla mentioned we should have a bachelorette party, yet I'm not allowed to arrange that myself," Lauren explains as she joins her hand with the other on her champagne flute stem.

"Yeah, because otherwise we would end up all watching a documentary in our pajamas," Layla refutes.

I smile and touch Lauren's arm to reassure her. "I would love to help, and we can make it elegant yet fun."

Suddenly all the men arrive to join us, and my stomach flutters when Wes joins us too.

"Man of the night," Cole congratulates Wes who comes to stand next to me.

"Did good, big brother. I hope this means I get a lifetime discount here," Sadie teases Wes as he grabs a fresh drink from the waiter.

"I'll consider it, depending on if your husband gets me those box seats at the Bears games," Wes retorts.

"Well played, my man." Logan toasts Wes.

I love that Wes is standing next to me, but it is excruciating at the same time. I want so desperately to grab his fingers and interlace them with my own. And I want to kiss his cheek like every other woman in this group circle can do, as they can show public affection.

Even if I change my mind, tonight is all Wes. Nothing should take away the attention that Jupiter deserves.

Everyone starts to talk, but I'm able to hear Wes mutter in my direction, "I need to talk with you."

"Oh, sure—"

The photographer interrupts us and indicates with his hands if he can take our group photo. Soon, we are all scrunching together, and Wes's hand lands on my lower back, sending a tingle to *all* parts of my body.

Wes takes full advantage of the situation and pulls me closer to his body under the pretense of the photo, but I feel it in my bones that it's to feel me close. To taunt me with his scent and feel his pulse beating.

Then I cling to him a little extra too.

And we stand there a few seconds longer until Charlie grabs Wes's attention from the side.

"I'll find you, okay?" Wes quickly says before following Charlie.

DURING DINNER, I got caught up in helping Reggie dress a few dessert plates and then I doubled-checked that we had extra gift bags by the valet. Wes was constantly in conversation with someone, and Sadie mentioned a few of his old business associates from Detroit were here. But then again, who wasn't here? Even a few hockey players stopped by.

This. Is. The. New. Hotspot.

"Hanging in there, Charlie?" I ask him as I come to stand

next to him in the corner of the bar area. He looks utterly exhausted.

"Yeah, it's a good adrenaline. We only get tonight once," he replies, and I like his answer.

"So true. Seems like people are starting to head out."

"Luckily, we'll do clean-up tomorrow. We aren't opening for lunch tomorrow, only dinner. We figured we would all need a sleep-in."

I let a yawn escape me. "Good plan. I guess this is when Wes kind of steps back since you're managing all the operations from here on out?"

Charlie can't help but grin, excited. "I mean, it's Wes, so he will still check in more than he needs to, but yeah, I think he trusts me enough to run a smooth ship. Plus, I can only imagine he's already eyeing his next project."

"Probably, he always has plans," I answer, and in that moment, I realize that I haven't seen Wes in a while. The whole night he keeps appearing only in the corner of my eye. "By any chance have you seen Wes lately?"

Charlie shrugs a shoulder. "Not since he went to talk with Kenzie. He's probably upstairs in his office for a breather. Would need that after talking to her."

"Kenzie?" I'm totally lost.

"Yeah, she's a blogger. Has a really big blog about best places to eat and shop in the city. Her following is actually quite impressive, but she can be a little, well… much."

It strikes me as odd that he would know this, as he doesn't strike me as someone who cruises on social media. "Right."

"I think she and Wes dated for a little while. Strange, too, as I wouldn't say she's really his type."

Oh, fuck. This doesn't feel great.

"Well, I will go see if I can find Wes then." I pretend to be casual but quickly find myself bolting away.

Heading upstairs, I feel on edge, and I don't really have any reason to be, but as I approach Wes's office with the door open, I freeze when I see Wes turning his head as the woman who I can only assume is Kenzie kisses him. Or tries. Or I don't know, as my eyes go blurry, I swear.

This is déjà vu. I've been in this situation before with Wes. Although last time it was innocent, this time I literally just watched the blond bombshell plant her lips on him.

"What are you doing?" he tells her and steps back, but she only moves closer to him, causing him to duck to the side.

"But you're single, I'm single. We had a few good dates. So why not try again?"

"Because..."

It makes me walk closer to his office door. I've never felt like a bear needing to mark my territory, but I feel it now. A territorial claim that I need to make clear to the other.

"Is it because of the event planner? I saw the way you keep glancing at her."

"Yes. It's because of Emily. We're together," he replies.

Stepping into the doorway, my appearance causes them both to look at me.

My stomach feels nauseous from this scene. I'm going to assume it's what my eyes witnessed and not the fact I'm birth control irresponsible. Wes never mentioned Kenzie once, except that I shouldn't contact those few bloggers in yellow...

Right. Now I know why.

"Emmy, how long have you been standing there?" Wes has a pained look as he steps into the middle of the room, waiting for my reaction.

"Long enough," is all I manage to respond.

I've never moved so fast in my life. "Emmy, wait!" I plead as I watch her walk away. Then I grab her arm to stop her before she can head toward the stairs. "It isn't what you think."

Her head is facing me, but her eyes avoid me.

"It wasn't last time either," she mumbles, and it dawns on me a year ago when, coincidently, another ex appeared right when Emily and I were about to head somewhere.

"I didn't kiss her. She tried, and I was having none of it." I have to start somewhere in the explanation of this colossal fuck-up.

Her sunken eyes glance briefly at me. "Why didn't you tell me your ex would be here?"

"She isn't an ex. It was two or three dates, a few months ago. Truthfully, it didn't cross my mind enough because it isn't a big deal. I thought we parted amicably, so it didn't seem strange when she wanted to come to the opening, it's her job."

"If it's not a big deal then why didn't you just mention it

to me at any point in the last month? Her name was on the damn list." Emily's brows arch up and she gives me a stern look.

My hands plant on both of her arms to encourage her to grasp my words. "You are completely right, and I'm sorry."

"You also just told her that you and I are together." I can't read her look.

But I'm now slightly stung, and I scoff in annoyance before my voice goes agitated. "Really? That's also an issue right now in this situation?"

"No. It's just… I'm confused right now." Her eyes blink several times then she steps out of my reach and holds her palm up.

We both stand there, saying nothing.

Emily shakes her head, and she seems to be thinking about something, then she nods and rubs her temples. "Okay. This is what we're going to do." Now she seems to be in action mode. "This is a big night for you, Wes. No matter what just went down, I can't let you end this as a bad night. So, I'm going to head downstairs and finish some things up with Charlie then head home. We can't have this conversation now. You and I can talk *tomorrow*."

She's putting up a wall between us, and I hate that. But she is being the sensible one between us so I have to trust that I shouldn't push this subject right now.

Once again, I try to reach for her hand, but she jolts it away when I almost nab it.

"Tomorrow, okay?" Her face is red, and I swear she's fighting back tears.

My own heart feels like it was stabbed.

"How about I come to your place later tonight?" I try my luck.

She shakes her head as her bottom lip trembles. "Tomorrow."

"Emmy, don't be upset. Nothing happened." My hands make fists at my sides, as I feel frustration needing to get out.

She glances at me once before turning to leave, taking every fiber of my heart with her.

———

THE NEXT MORNING, I'm at Emily's front door at 9am. After last night, I couldn't sleep a wink. I probably should have texted her, but I couldn't wait any longer.

But she doesn't let me pass through the doorway when I arrive. Instead, she leans against the doorframe with arms crossed, in jeans and a t-shirt, and her eyes tell me she didn't get much sleep either.

"Can I come in?" I ask and rub the stubble on my chin.

"I'm not sure that's a good idea." At least she sounds like she has calmed down a little.

"Is it really that bad?" The fear can possibly be heard in my voice.

Emily bites her lip before pulling her hair up into a messy ponytail. "I'm not sure I'll be strong enough if you come in; you have this knack at getting me naked when I should be furious." A faint smirk toys at the corner of her mouth.

"Sounds like a perfect plan."

"No. Maybe. Well, no. I think a little time and distance will be good for us." She looks up at me to search for my reaction.

Never saw this suggestion coming, nor am I thrilled. "Horrible idea," I snap back.

It only makes her smirk grow. "I knew you would say

that, but Wes, I do think it would be good for us to cool down from this for a few days. I need it to make sure I'm thinking clearly."

I feel like this is about more than last night. "About what?"

"A lot of things. Us."

My eyes shoot up to her and instantly she continues.

"Actually, since the opening was supposed to be the last event I arrange for you then I have a few days off, so I'll head to Boston to tie up some loose ends... Space. It'll be good."

I rub my forehead and a feeling of pure annoyance hits me. My hand lands against the wall next to the door, making her startle. "You always do this. Last year you did the same. *You* are the one who put the brakes on us and said it was better that way."

Her hand flies to her hip. "Are you kidding me right now? I thought we both agreed it was for the best."

"Yeah, a year later when we discussed it," I remind her matter-of-factly.

"Unbelievable." She seems fuming mad. "We wouldn't even be in this situation if *you* didn't put on the brakes when I said, 'please, Wes, please take me in the back of your car like any normal college guy would because they think it's a grand idea.'" She's sassy as she mocks me, that's for sure.

"Are we really having this ridiculous conversation?" I shake my head slightly.

"I don't even know. Look…" She rubs her temples. "We both need to cool off."

I look at her and hate to admit her idea is smart. I also sense there is something else but can't pinpoint what.

"I don't want to upset you. I came here to do the opposite. I can't change your mind?"

"Already found a flight for later today," she answers simply.

I respond instantly, "I'll come with."

Her face stays neutral. "No, Wes, I really need some air."

"What's going on, Emmy? Is this really all about last night?"

She gives me a hopeless look, and I wonder what she is debating to say.

We both stand there in her doorway in a sort of standoff. I know she's going to win, because I'll do anything for her, and some strange feeling inside me has me believing everything she does is for me, she always wants the best for me.

"I'm serious about us. You and me. It's our time," I remind her of what I said yesterday, and I reach out to caress her cheek. It causes her the catch her breath and close her eyes gently. But I have to put my foot down, I can only be so patient. "No more talking when you're back. It's decision time. I'll give you space but that's the deal. We both know what we want."

"Okay," she answers softly. "Give me a week. We'll talk next Sunday."

"That's a whole damn week, not a few days."

"What's a week if our decision is about a lifetime?" she counters, and I know she isn't going to budge.

She places her hand on top of mine on her face as we both stare at one another in this moment.

And it's the scariest thing I have ever done, but I kiss her cheek in agreement and walk away. I trust her with my life and, hell, my heart included. I have to believe she won't let it go.

———

"So, you've been together the past few weeks? It wasn't just sleeping together after the wedding? I mean, you were both kind of obvious, but I like to hear the confirmation." Logan passes me a beer bottle then leans back on his sofa at his place.

Using my keychain, I snap the cap of my beer off. "Yeah, we've always kind of had this thing between us, it's just never been the right time."

"Until now. She'll come around, and space can be good. I believe you and I met when Sadie and I were on a pause."

I sneer that he could even compare. "You were totally in the doghouse and my sister wanted nothing to do with you, yet still you asked for my help. I would like to think things aren't that bad for me."

Logan grins as he throws his feet on top of his coffee table. "My point is that people realize a lot when you don't see one another for even a few days."

"I know. Emily and I have had that happen a few times to us." It's just the last time, a year ago, when I saw her and kissed her and pinned her against a brick wall, it drove me crazy. It's lingered in my mind since.

Truth be told, I was on a date a few months back with Kenzie when Sadie texted me that she was excited that Emily would be moving back to Chicago. Immediately, my mind flooded with a possibility, and I ended things with Kenzie right then and there. I didn't even know if Emily was single, but I didn't care. Even if she had some guy with a Boston accent, I knew I would pursue her.

"It'll be okay. Mark my words, this time next week this will be a distant memory."

The sound of Sadie entering the penthouse reminds me that I haven't talked to her about Emily yet. Emmy wanted to do that.

Sadie emerges from the hall with a few grocery bags. "Husband, I'm home," she chimes with a wide smile then sees me and frowns. "Brother, I'm home." Immediately she drops the bags to the floor and flops onto the sofa next to Logan.

She crosses her arms, looks at me, and waits for me to talk.

"Yes?" I ask.

"Something you would like to share?" she asks as she grabs a throw pillow to cuddle with.

"Maybe now isn't the time," Logan attempts to intervene.

My sister gives him a daggered stare and he backs down because the man will do anything to appease her, and since it's for my sister then I can't tell him to grow a pair either. Sadie returns her gaze to me with a thrown-on smile.

"I just need one of you to confirm what I know. Just one of you. You or Emily, anyone." She holds up her finger.

For the first time in a day, I feel like I can manage a half-smile.

"Do you have a view on it?" I throw back at her.

"Yes, I do. Strong views of the positive variety, but I am not sure we should talk about this since Emily seemed kind of distant by text yesterday. She didn't say why but I assumed you messed up somehow."

I pinch the bridge of my nose. "Thanks. Your confidence is oh, so sincere." My sarcasm tolerance today is on low.

Sadie throws the pillow at me. "I'm not worried." That spikes some hope in me. "Just give her the space. You know Ems, she likes to be alone and mind map her life with highlighters and a posterboard. In the meantime, keep yourself busy. I already saw some early reviews and they're stellar."

"She's right," Logan adds. "I've already asked my secretary to book all my business lunches at Jupiter."

"Even that blogger who you dated was positive," Sadie speaks as she scrolls on her phone.

This grabs my attention in a heartbeat and my head jerks up to look at Sadie. "Wait, what?"

"You haven't seen?" Sadie holds her phone out to me, and I see the title of the post about opening night at Jupiter. Dread hits me when I see that Kenzie wrote—although positive—a remark about Emily.

Emily Cates really brought the opening to life with her attention to the small details that made every aspect of Jupiter a cause for festivity. It's clear her passion in the planning came from a desire to celebrate the future success of Jupiter that is owned by her boyfriend, Weston Bay.

Fuck me, the last thing Emmy wanted. The whole point of waiting to tell people was to avoid this, and now I see exactly where her mind frame came from.

Before my sigh can fully escape, my phone vibrates. I pull it from my jeans and swipe to answer. "Hey, Charlie… Yeah, I'll be in later today then maybe I'm out of town for a day. An old buddy from Detroit has a potential property for me to check out to invest in… Uh, yeah, Emily should be back in a few days… She's in Boston… Wait, what do you mean?" I ask.

"I thought she wasn't interested in that job opportunity in Boston. I was with her when she got an e-mail from an old colleague about a job," Charlie explains from the other end of the line, and another wave of fear hits me.

"Oh. Right," is all I manage before tying up the call. I'm now even more confused, as she already started everything to work freelance here. No way would the other night have made her change her mind, right? Looking at Logan, I ask, "Do you have another beer? No, scratch that, can we have a whiskey?"

"Shit. That bad?" Logan gets up from the couch and heads to his alcohol supply in the corner of the living room.

There is no way.

Nope. I'm not letting her slip away.

EMILY

I look into the hotel mirror as I rub the back of my neck. Who knew closing a bank account could take so long? The first five minutes was about *why* I was closing, the next five minutes was the lady behind the computer trying to upsell me on new products, then finally twenty minutes later, they had me fill out ten pieces of paper to close the damn bank account.

Grabbing my toothbrush, I notice my pack of birth control pills and instantly my stomach drops at that reminder. Add a post-it to the life plan that includes what not to do when you get sidetracked—miss not only one, but three pills. Needless to say, it's the tip of the iceberg.

Space and clearing my head seemed like the only viable option I could think of. My brain had the idea that I made the right decision by saying we both need a breather. Plus, I don't want to tell Wes anything until I know for sure, and it's too early for me to confirm. Otherwise, he may also freak out, and two of us freaking out isn't going to help either of us.

In a way, staring at a hotel ceiling is what I need right now. My mind is a bit all over the place. I know Wes wasn't intentionally trying to hurt me, but things took a turn for us in the span of ten minutes and my brain didn't know how to process the repeat of the scene with Wes. I didn't want to overreact, but I didn't want to brush everything under the rug either.

Would much rather be at home, eating ice cream and allowing myself some wallow time. In the past two days, I have read all of Jupiter's reviews and they are exactly what they should be—five star. I laughed at the scowl on Wes's face in a photograph accompanying an article about the man behind the new restaurant; the photographer was aiming for determined and hot—I think. Then I cringed when I saw Kenzie's blog post. Go figure someone who tried to kiss your non-public boyfriend could write such kind words about you.

My phone vibrates next to the sink, and I see it's Sadie, so I jab my index finger to accept the video call.

"Hey, Sadie," I say as I grab my toothbrush.

"Hey, how are things?" I can hear she's afraid to ask.

"Just ask, Sadie," I urge her as I search for my toothpaste.

"So, a call isn't ideal to do this, but it's kind of out there that you and Wes, well…"

I give up on the toothbrush and toothpaste and head back into the bedroom where I collapse on the bed and hold the phone above me. Sadie seems to be in her bed with fluffy pajamas on.

"Sorry I didn't tell you."

She smiles softly at me. "We should probably talk about that in person, but I think it's better that you didn't tell me."

"How so?"

Her smile widens. "I always wanted you both together, but I didn't want to know until it was a sure thing. I think I still don't want to know until you both tell me it's a sure and forever thing. Otherwise, I'll only get my hopes up."

I lie there and my mouth quirks at her logic. It also makes me slightly relieved that she would be excited for me; I was never sure where she would stand. A month ago, she made me scared she wouldn't be happy about it. Now I feel like she would be on board. Except, in this very moment, there isn't much to tell, as Wes and I are on a pause, and telling Sadie that I may be knocked up by her brother seems like a bleak option too.

"Well, then we should probably stop talking about this. I kind of freaked out and asked for some space from Wes."

"It happens sometimes," she assures me and pulls her blanket higher.

"You okay? You look kind of sick," I observe.

"Totally. Just tired, and Logan has late meetings, but I was wondering if you would come for dinner when you're back, maybe on the weekend?"

"As in you and me?" I'm trying to sus out any potential ploys.

"Yeah, maybe Ruby too. Logan is out for a guys' night, and relax, I don't even think Wes will be there, as he's in Detroit on business."

This surprises me, and it's also complete news too. "Really? What's he doing there?"

"Something about a new property or restaurant. Will you bring dessert?"

"Sure." I nod, but inside, my head questions what this tidbit of information could mean.

Sadie and I wrap up our call quite quickly, but I don't leave my position on the bed. I'm like a comatose person, exhausted and unsure if I should reach out to Wes now to pick up our conversation or to fulfill my curiosity about what he's up to.

Blowing out a breath, I decide to wait. Clearly Wes also

has things to think about if he's contemplating Michigan again. Maybe he is re-evaluating what he wants. Part of me feels like I'm being irrational, because I can't stand the thought that I may have just pushed Wes away instead of giving us air to make sure we're on the same page for a future with one another—together.

———

I'VE JUST ARRIVED at Sadie and Logan's place, and I set the cherry cobbler that I picked up from the bakery down on the counter. I look up at Sadie cooking in the kitchen, an apron thrown on to really make her look like a 1950s housewife. Whereas I am in a buttoned-down sweater dress and tights.

"I am not even going to ask what would possess you to make all this food." I'm almost dazed by the number of offerings splayed out.

"I thought we could live it up like we used to when we always made snack plates and had wine." She slides a glass of wine my way, which I can thankfully drink since I confirmed a giant bullet dodged this morning, avoiding one crisis.

I focus on Sadie checking on something in the oven. "Need a hand?" I offer.

"Sure, could you mix the salad?" Sadie speaks as she cuts into the roast chicken in front of her.

"Mission accepted," I confirm as I set my glass down and reach for the salad bowl filled with a bag of lettuce. Pulling the bowl to me, I begin to work on the salad. "Ruby is coming, right?"

Right on cue, Ruby announces her arrival, as she must have let herself in. "The party is here." She places a bottle of tequila on the kitchen island.

"A relaxed ladies' night in," Sadie states as she stares at the bottle, petrified.

"I mean, I guess I could do one shot." I shrug, and Ruby winks at me in approval.

As Sadie returns to cooking, I grab Ruby's attention as she takes her jacket off and places it on the back of the chair. "Sorry I never got back to you. I've been… all over the place."

"I know." She steals my glass of wine for a sip. "But it's okay, my issue is resolved."

"What issue is that?"

Ruby taps the glass with her dark fingernails. "It's, well… you know what, it doesn't matter. I'll tell you another day, as I may need your help with something." She shakes it off.

"You sure?"

"About as sure as you keep trying to avoid the main topic of conversation this evening." She cocks her head at me.

Sadie turns, pointing a baster at me. "Exactly. Let's get the food on the table, then we talk."

I roll my eyes. I know there's no way to avoid this. A few minutes later, we're all settled with food on plates, wine in glasses, and eyes staring at Sadie.

"You're not drinking?" I ask, slightly perplexed.

"Oh, ugh, no. Got medicine for my allergies," Sadie explains as she stuffs a big spoonful of salad on her plate.

"It's allergy season?" Ruby asks, not quite buying the explanation.

"Hamster… Logan's nephew has a hamster… yep, and he comes to visit when Mason visits, so who knew you could be allergic to hamsters. Anyhow, diversion done. Tell me, Emily, how is it sleeping with my brother and not telling me?" Sadie drinks from her glass of water with a straight face. Ruby just huffs out a laugh.

Swallowing a piece of bread, I put my roll down. "Where do you want me to begin?"

A warm smile spreads partially on Sadie's face. "It started when you began working for him?"

"Yeah, I mean, at your wedding."

"And a year ago," Ruby mutters, and I gently kick her under the table.

Sadie's jaw drops softly. "There's more history?"

Drinking from my wine, I'm relieved to finally lay this on the table. "Before I went off to college, Wes and I were just kind of there and we got close."

"But that's when you started to hate him." Sadie looks at me blankly.

"I never hated him, and don't make me go into all the details, but it just didn't… I don't know. Didn't end smoothly." I take another drink of wine.

"Want that shot of tequila now or shall I tell her about the time you and Wes were all over one another in a club?" Ruby flashes me an overdone smile.

"What? You knew and didn't tell me?" Sadie snaps her head in Ruby's direction.

Ruby shrugs. "Girl Scout's honor code. Plus, it wasn't my place to say."

"It was a year ago… again, didn't end smoothly," I add and debate if tequila is looking like a good option.

There's a long pause that graces the table, and I wonder what Sadie is thinking, but then the corners of her mouth crack and curve up.

"My instinct about you two recently was right. Okay, so now?" she asks and stuffs her mouth with a forkful of casserole.

"A slight mess. I saw Kenzie try to kiss him and then I

kind of snapped for several reasons and said we both should take some space before doing anything else."

"That's braver than me," Ruby notes and pours some shots.

"Trust me, I needed the space. My week has been unusual. We agreed to meet tomorrow and talk… well, I think we did. We haven't been in contact." I realize I am petrified for what tomorrow may bring.

"It was obvious at my wedding and Jupiter's opening night that you two are into each other. My parents even asked if there was something going on." Sadie smiles to herself, and in that moment, I realize that Wes confided in me information that Sadie doesn't know about her parents. My loyalty feels tested, but it's not my place or desire to break Wes's trust.

"It was more than obvious; their sexual tension made me feel like I needed to throw a condom at them," Ruby quips.

Sadie rolls her eyes at Ruby, "Classy," then returns her gaze to me. "So, what will you tell Wes tomorrow?"

The sound of the front door opening and a herd of people entering breaks our conversation. We all watch the people coming in. Logan, Cole, Noah… and Wes.

My body tightens and my heart may explode. I wasn't expecting to see him. He doesn't notice me, as he's laughing with Cole who has a case of beer in hand.

"What's this?" Sadie asks as Logan comes to lean down to kiss her.

"The bar was packed and the Michigan-Purdue game is on. We decided to come back during halftime to finish it here. I figured you would have lots of food," Logan explains as he rubs Sadie's cheek affectionately with his thumb.

"I know, but I thought it was guys' night… *away* from here," she mutters through her tight-lipped smile.

Logan looks around the table then double-takes between

Wes and me. "Oh. *Ohh.* Right, well, I think we can all appreciate that the game is on?"

"Absolutely," I say. I meet Wes's beautiful eyes. We don't blink or say anything. The commotion in my chest feels almost impossible to control. He's surprised to see me, and the feeling is mutual. We were both anticipating tomorrow.

Sadie claps her hands together. "Okay, so who wants dinner?"

This dinner may require the whole damn bottle of tequila.

● 23

EMILY

"This is okay, right?" Wes double-checks with me before taking the seat next to me. The sound of plates being added to the table and food being served is in the background.

I set my wine glass down. "For sure." Sounded totally unbelievable, and his humored look supports that fact.

A soft smile toys on his mouth. "You're wearing my bracelet."

My heart flutters the way he looks at me so fondly. "I… haven't taken it off." His smile is subtle before we both turn to focus on the others.

"Hear you're going to help with our wedding planning." Noah smiles at me, and I'm happy he is unknowingly distracting me from staring at Wes and surveying his every inch.

Turning to Noah, I nod. "Yeah, Lauren asked, and I'm so excited. We'll meet next week about planning… you're part of that meeting too, in case you were wondering." I wink.

Cole pipes in. "Nah. My sister can call the shots, let's not pretend Noah has a say."

"You never stop, do you?" Noah asks him, and I can see it's all lighthearted.

"For you? Never," Cole replies before drinking from his beer bottle.

"Are you going to do kids' parties? My nephew has insane birthdays," Logan mentions.

Circling my wine glass with the edge with my finger, I contemplate. "I don't know. I mean, only if I know the people, otherwise I'm not sure I have it in me energy-wise."

"But everything local? Here in Chicago?" Wes seems to check, and I look at him, confused.

"Yes. Why wouldn't it be?"

"Not in Boston?" he counters.

"No. Why would you think that?" I wonder, and I see he has something on his mind. "What about Michigan? Are *you* doing everything local, here in Chicago?" I realize we're both challenging each other over information that I'm not sure either of us knows.

"What do you mean?" Wes now looks baffled.

The hushed debate between Cole and Ruby interrupts us, and we all draw our attention to them.

"Anybody want more chicken?" Sadie asks, oblivious.

"What's going on with you two?" Logan studies Cole and Ruby.

The table goes quiet as we all hear the tail end of their conversation. "We have to tell them," Ruby admits and nudges Cole's arm.

"Sure. Why not." He sounds unenthused. "Ems, can you add us to your calendar for a wedding reception?"

Someone drops a fork to their plate, causing the sound to fill the dead-silent room.

"Uhm, okay." I don't know how to answer, as I try to figure out what the hell is going on. "For who?"

Ruby pours a shot of tequila. "For us."

"As in you and…" Logan can't grasp this news.

Cole takes the shot of tequila and downs it. "Ruby and me."

Everyone's eyes bug out and the room is so silent you could hear a pin drop.

"Since when?" I can't help but try to figure out these facts.

"It's new," Ruby confirms.

"We could have the party at Jupiter, right?" Cole casually asks Wes. "Wow, this salad looks delicious." Cole continues on as if nothing just happened and dives his fork into the greens.

"I, uh, should we do dessert? Yeah, let's do dessert," Sadie speaks from utter shock.

———

I PUT the cobbler in the oven to warm it up while my head wraps around the latest gossip. The heat hits me as I use the kitchen towel to take hold of the tray. I'm too busy focusing on the oven to look behind me when I feel someone's presence.

"You bent over is always a good look," a confident voice informs me. The sound of Wes's voice startles me. So much so that I lose my grip on the tray.

"Fuck," I cry out, as the burning strike against the skin of my hand is brief but not brief enough. The sound of the metal tray falling to the floor fills the room.

"Shit." Wes quickly comes to me then follows me to the kitchen sink where he turns the faucet on. "Totally my fault, I shouldn't have snuck up on you."

I place my hand under the stream of lukewarm water. "What the hell, Wes. Where did you come from?"

"I'm sorry, let me look," he requests as his fingertips gently grab my wrist and guide my hand into a better view. His touch causes more heat to my senses than the burn.

"You okay? There's a first-aid kit in the laundry room," Sadie tells me as she grabs some plates.

"Come on, I'll help you." Wes indicates his head to the hall, and I follow.

Arriving in the laundry room, he reaches for a box above the sink as I take a seat on the low bench and watch as he studies the various tubes of ointment. I notice the slim fit of his dark jeans and navy-blue buttoned shirt today, which isn't helping my nerves. When his eyes turn to me, I notice they almost glint, and a throbbing in my chest forms for a second.

"Found it." He kneels down in front of me and grabs my arm. His smell keeps me alert. It's subtle but sharp, with hints of spring fresh.

"You're not in Michigan?"

His eyes peer up to meet mine. "I came back early. I was only there to check out a property for a silent investment."

"But you would stay here?" I pry.

"Yeah. You? Any job opportunities in Boston come up?"

The cold feeling from the gel hits my skin, and it makes me angry in a way, because it means I can't fully feel the touch of his fingers on me. Looking at his fingers massaging ointment onto the back of my hand, the image sends a tingle though my body. The sound of his name alone always influences me. This situation only multiplies it.

"No, why did you ask earlier?"

"Charlie mentioned you had a job opportunity." He doesn't look at me, and it dawns on me that I told Charlie about the e-mail.

"True, but I have zero interest in it. Literally just went to Boston to close my bank account and pick up some old mail."

He sighs in relief, and his fingers linger longer than needed on my skin. Our eyes meet, and the silence isn't helping the tension in this small laundry room.

"How are you?" he asks softly, and his tone tells me he doesn't mean in this moment, he means this week.

A faint, lined smile forms on my face. "Not great, and you?"

"The same. Guess you couldn't really avoid me in this situation, needed me to save you." I hear the effort to tease me, but it falls flat.

He looks to his finger that begins to draw a circle on the back of my hand. Wes swallows and he returns his gaze to me.

"I think you can let my hand go now."

He doesn't let go.

"You don't want me to." He sounds very sure of himself.

I shake my head gently. "Wes." His name escapes me as a whispered plea, but I have to react with an almost bashful look.

"Look at me, Emmy," he requests as he moves his hand so his long finger can hook under my chin to guide my gaze to him.

My head moves again in his path, and before I can decide what to do, his mouth covers my own. Our lips seal together for a firm, hard kiss that I've missed the last few days. Our connection at the mouth lingers as our lips brush each other's to take a breath, before we kiss again.

This time his arms encircle around me, pulling me tight to him, causing me to warm all over and loop my arms around his neck, as I want our bodies flush together. My greedy mouth demands more from him and he kisses me harder. A wildfire between us is quickly blazing.

It's not long until he picks me up, and my legs wrap around his waist until he lands me on top of the washing machine. Now we're at an even better angle to press our middles together and feel our need in this moment. So lost in one another, we're oblivious to our roaming hands and bodies moving in a frenzy. It causes the machine to turn on as we accidently hit a button on the screen, which in turn makes us look at one another and at the same moment laugh.

Our noses nuzzle as he suggests, "We should get out of here. This night is all forms of strange."

"You mean Cole and Ruby or that your sister's expecting?" I prompt the obvious.

He looks at me oddly.

"You haven't noticed your sister's lack of drinking that she blames on hamster allergies?"

"What do you mean? I had a hamster as a kid and she was fine, petrified of the thing but no allerg—" It dawns on him. "Christ, she's really hopping onto the housewife train." He rubs his forehead as he takes in the news.

"Everyone has life-changing news, and I'm literally getting a headache from this night... I wasn't expecting to see you until tomorrow," I admit.

"We need to get out of here, Emmy. Come home with me?" His eyes pierce mine with lust, and he seems so determined that I don't have a chance to say no. He steps back and offers me his hand to hop off the machine. "We said we would talk tomorrow. So tonight, we don't need to say anything." His words are fueled with heat and that tint of resolve again.

Taking his hand, I don't answer, but I do root my feet to the floor. His arm snakes around me and urges me forward.

Wes leans down to breathe close to my ear. "Best part about this crazy night is nobody will notice that we're getting out of here *now*."

The thought of the plans in his head awakens all my molecules. I don't want to talk tonight anyway.

Even though we should.

WE SNEAK out of Sadie and Logan's place, which is easily done with a night like tonight. Wes and I don't speak as we walk back to his place, as he only lives a few blocks from Sadie's. Instead, the tension between us is thick, and every step closer is upping the ante.

But the moment we step into the elevator, everything evaporates. Our mouths meet instantly, and our hands roam, and the man actually starts unzipping my jacket with an impatience that in return makes me want to do the same. By the time he unlocks his front door and we flood into his place, we both have scraps of clothing hanging off our bodies.

Wes walks me backward and his kisses tell me he needs something tonight. Our throaty sounds are constant until he shuts me up by pressing me against the wall and covering my mouth completely with his own, his tongue transmitting a message that he will lead us.

His hands grip the line of buttons on my dress, and in a quick jerk, he rips the dress open, causing buttons to pop off.

Holy hell, he is hot tonight.

"You owe me a dress," I purr.

A sinful chuckle escapes from the back of his throat as his hands roam the waist of my tights. "I'll owe you these too." In a swift movement he pushes them down and causes them to rip too.

The whole move causes me to sizzle with want.

"Open your legs wide for me, baby," he murmurs against my skin. His hand urges my thighs to part, and they easily do.

Before I can think, his fingers disappear and rub against the cotton, causing my eyes to hood closed and my head to fall back.

This is what I need. Moments of complete focus on our bodies, no thoughts or discussion involved.

"Wes, take me to your bed," I gasp as I grip his shoulders.

He answers by swinging an arm under my knees then carrying me down his hall. The whole time my eyes peer up and admire his face. It's only been a week, but I've missed touching his face, and that stubble, so perfect to feel against my skin.

Wes lays me on top of his mattress before discarding his clothes, and I work on my bra.

We move with speed to quickly be able to kiss again and run our mouths along necks, shoulders, and any body part that we want in this chaotic need. In a swift jolt, he guides my body to sit on top of him. His warm body instantly like a blanket as he wraps his arms around me, except for the cool air that hits my aching nipples. But that isn't for long, as his mouth covers the hardened bud, making my body arch into him.

Ragged breathing follows us as we explore each other, trying to get everything at once. A mess of hands and starving mouths.

Wes slows his trail of kisses along my collarbone and up my neck. "I need to take you, Emmy."

I respond with a nod before he slowly lays me back with my legs wrapped around his waist.

With eyes holding, he drives himself inside of me until he

is planted deep within to the fullest. Our moans intertwine as my head nestles into his neck.

Suddenly our crazed passion surrenders to the need to move slowly, in sync, and together in more tender thought.

He pulls me closer to his body as I milk him tighter and let him guide my rolling hips.

"Tomorrow, Emmy, you better be here. Because this is our future. This, every damn day, until one day I am your husband, and then in a few years, the father of your children. You're the one," he says through heavy breath, twinned with a low growl.

"Wes," I cry out before gently biting into the flesh of his shoulder as his words hit me at the very moment he touches that spot within me that sends me seeing stars, and it's now combined with his words that stick to my heart.

He rolls us until we're on our sides and he pins me down with our interlaced hands landing above me on the pillow.

"Say nothing more, Emmy. Just show me. Show me how much you want me in this moment, and tomorrow, be here." He speaks softly against the skin of my neck.

I barely nod, as I am so lost in lust, in him, in us.

Instead, I tilt my body to collide with him as closely as possible.

Because tomorrow, this will all be different.

24

WES

My eyes slowly open as my body stretches in bed, the morning sun peeking through the curtains and causing me to blink. It only takes two blinks before I remember the fact that I fell asleep with Emmy in my bed where she belongs. Then my mind registers that I also gave her an ultimatum.

No more circles. No more games. It's now or never between us.

Rolling over, I expect to see her lying there sound asleep. Hopefully because she fell asleep having made a decision, the right decision.

My chest aches the moment my hand reaches for the vacant cold spot on the sheets and realize that she isn't here. Immediately, I am fully awake and pop up to sitting. Looking frantically around, I see that her clothes are no longer scattered on my floor.

An emotional hurricane brews inside me, and my fist hits the mattress with force to let out some frustration. How could she walk away from us?

Everything we want is for our taking.

Crawling out of bed, I quickly grab a pair of boxers from the drawer then head to the kitchen via the hall. All the while, hoping I'll run into Emily. Maybe she woke up early. Every step becomes more treacherous as I realize she is nowhere in my apartment.

Sighing, I walk to the window to look out at the morning light. It's going to be a cold day, as autumn is picking up. Fucking fitting, since my heart is feeling pretty cold all of the sudden.

She made her choice.

The wrong choice.

It takes a few minutes for me to realize that I'll drive myself crazy if I stay here all morning. I can either find Emily to figure out why she doesn't want to take the chance or keep myself busy and learn to let it all go, which even I know may take months or possibly years. Hell, a fucking lifetime.

Heading to my bathroom, I turn the faucet on to the shower. The quick hot shower does little to improve my mood. This is not how this morning was supposed to go. There should be another body rubbing against me, sharing this water, then we would lie in bed all morning and talk about a future.

After changing and looking in the kitchen to realize I'm all out of coffee, I grab my keys and my jacket. The moment I open my front door, I freeze.

Emily is standing there balancing a tray of coffees in one hand, a paper bag under the same arm, and she's searching in her bag for something. She looks up with the most elated smile that I have seen on a woman, and she wears it well.

"Oh, hey! I was trying to find your key; I took the spare one to let myself back in." She gives up on the search.

I stand there, confused and entirely puzzled. "What do you mean?"

I'm still blocking the door, so she stands in front of me with a bewildered look. "I thought I had at least another half-hour before you would wake so I thought I would grab some coffee and donuts to surprise you with breakfast in bed, but I had to wait an extra ten minutes because your crullers weren't quite ready—"

"Wait. You went to get us breakfast?" I'm trying to register this information.

Lines form on her forehead. "Uhm, yeah. Where do you think…?" It hits her where my mind went. "You thought I wouldn't want this?"

"I may have thought about it for a second." She doesn't need to know that I was about to have a full-on end-of-the-world meltdown. Internally, relief spreads, and excitement begins to jump around in my stomach.

"I went to get us breakfast," she repeats softly with a frozen look.

"And this is the one time you chose not to use a post-it? I know you carry them around." I feel a grin forming.

"Figured after what we did in bed last night during round number three that you got the memo about how today was going to go." The corner of her mouth stretches. This woman makes a solid point.

Reaching out to her, my fingers claw the fabric of her jacket and pull her to me. "Your type of breakfast may need to wait. There is only one thing I want for breakfast." A devilish smirk begins to form on my face as I gently drag her into my place and kick the door closed with my foot.

Amazing how your day can go from zero to ten in a second.

She sets the tray of coffee and bag of donuts on the side table and unzips her coat before hanging it on the hook. I notice she's wearing one of my shirts which makes her twenty times hotter right now than she already was in my head.

"Can I have a shower first? I have literally been walking around with… well… you're still in me." She flashes me a playful look, which I would swear is a blush.

This makes me pull her flush to me and growl into her neck. "That's the way it should be. You're mine."

She squeals that adorable sound that makes my heart shake every time. The only way to calm me is by capturing her mouth with my own for a long, devouring kiss. The kiss grounds us back to focusing on the present.

"I guess another diversion in the bedroom has to wait, and we should finally talk like two normal humans who should maybe get an award for miscommunication?" I ask as I take her hands in mine and give them a kiss.

"That's probably the right plan. *So…* my week started out with a bang, remember?" She gives me a hopeless look before we walk to the sofa in my living room and sit down.

"You know nothing happened, and I am sorry—"

She holds a hand up to stop me then enters a rambling mode. "I know, but it wasn't great. Anyhow, I was overwhelmed and couldn't sleep, then I saw my post-it wall of to-do lists and the missing pills, then you showed up—"

I interrupt her. "What?" I blink several times, as she lost me already, yet I touch her arm to calm her.

Her face stills and her lips part. "*Oh*, it's nothing. I mean, it's not nothing, just in the end it led to nothing."

"So lost," I tell her blankly.

"I forgot a few of my birth control pills. It's so unlike me, I never forget. I'll be more careful, I promise."

Huh, that's news. She thought for a second she could have been pregnant. My mouth quirks out, and I feel my face squinch. For a second, I have a quick glimpse to the future, and it doesn't scare me one bit.

"You should have told me."

She gently shakes her head. "Relax, the last thing you needed was me informing you of a maybe situation on the night of your opening."

It dawns on me her logic and timeline, causing me to puff out a breath. "Christ, woman, you are amazing. I had no clue where your head was at then. I wish you'd told me, but you are slightly right too, that wasn't the best time for me. Yet, it wasn't the right time for you either." My thumb strokes the back of her hand. She is so selfless, and I love her even more. "Is that what was bothering you the most during the last week?"

"Yeah. Neither of us want a kid right now."

I lean in to kiss her forehead. "It doesn't matter, we're here now, and you have successfully opened *the* hot spot in the city," she tells me.

"Least you have some good reviews too?" I squeak out, and I'm kind of afraid to bring it up as I shrug.

In return she playfully hits me. "I guess. Can we just skip *that* topic altogether? It's done."

I'm relieved and in awe of how remarkable she is at getting us focused on what matters. "Say no more," I assure her. "You thought about us?"

She squeezes our joined hands, and her head retreats back slightly with a sparkle in her eyes. "I always do. I'm yours."

With one hand moving to frame her face, my other strokes her hair as her eyes stare into my own. "It took long enough," I remind her.

Emily smiles to herself as she thinks, making me wait for her to speak her mind. "You know, you and I... we don't have some tragic love story or major obstacles, never did... It was like we danced around one another and used the most ridiculous little things to keep us apart. I have life figured out. Even lately, saying you would sidetrack me was an excuse."

Her logic is our truth. "Sounds like that's our story and you do have it figured out."

"I do, and I think the reason it was that way was because I knew that you, Weston Bay, are not some distraction guy." She grabs my hands. "You're the *perfect* distraction... the only distraction I will ever want." Her eyes blaze with affection.

I lean in to give her a gentle peck on the lips. "Happy we realize that."

She laughs. "Who would have thought it would take you being my boss to get us there."

"So, when you mention I'm all that you'll ever want..." Her words hit me deep in the middle of my heart. "Ever? That's good, because I am not letting you go. You're what I want, what I need, who I love."

Her beaming smile spreads before she gives me a quick kiss on the lips then stands up and grabs my hand to tug me to follow her, glancing over her shoulder back at me.

I wrap my arms around her from behind as we walk toward my bedroom. But then, she abruptly stops and playfully swats my arms away. "I'm not letting you go," I repeat.

She gives me a warning glare. "Yes, you are. We both know we aren't leaving your bed this morning, and we'll need snacks in the form of donuts."

"You're right, and you know I'm going to lick every morsel off you." I let her go and she runs to grab the bag of donuts and double-takes when she looks at the coffees.

"We're past coffee, right?" she questions me with a cute look of doubt.

"I would think we're both wide awake now." I chuckle.

She nearly skips back to me, and we both head into my room and throw ourselves on my unmade bed. I grab the white paper bag from her hands, but she doesn't let me take the bag.

"Seriously, Wes, I'm famished. Between last night's dramatic dinner and the sex after, then the middle-of-the-night session, I can't anymore." She smiles drowsily.

"I would tell you to take your clothes off and I promise you can just relax, let me do all the work, but I can't have my girlfriend starving."

She grins as she peppers kisses around my face as we lie there on our sides. "Don't worry, I'm always ready for you."

Lying there, we both hold one another's face, enjoying this moment with our eyes locked, and I'm not sure why I haven't already told her the obvious, as we have both declared so much. "Emmy, I love you so fucking much."

"In case you missed all my indications about our future, I love you too," she answers, and we both lean in—ready to dive into this relationship, fearlessly.

And in such a happy state, she decides that we will be a good item on the breakfast menu to have first. The rest of the morning, we lie there talking about a future that is finally ours.

EPILOGUE: EMILY

A FEW MONTHS LATER

"Yeah, I am completely sure the cake needs to be delivered by 9am. If it's not, then I promise you I will be calling you at 9:01." I can get a little ruthless sometimes, but I run a tight ship.

Only a few months in and I have about two events every week. A mix of friends of friends, business associates of the guys, and people who hear about me through word of mouth.

Throwing my phone back into my bag, I stick my key into the front door of Wes's—well, *our* place as I carry the last small box of stuff under one arm.

Wes was adamant that I move in when my short-term lease was up, and there was no hesitation on my part, as most of my stuff had already migrated to his anyhow since we made a point to see each other every free night we had.

Walking through the front door, I set the box down then take off my winter coat. "Have my last box of stuff. I think it's going to snow," I mention as I place my coat on the hook.

Then I notice that the place is kind of dark and Wes hasn't greeted me. "Wes?"

"In here," I hear from the other room.

I walk through the hall to the open living room and kitchen area where I immediately stop in my tracks. There are candles everywhere like that picnic date night we had. My eyes don't need to scan far, as in the middle of the room is Wes, looking handsome with his dark blue button-down shirt and dark jeans. He's on one knee…

Oh. My. God.

"W-what are doing?" I stammer out as I slowly walk to him.

He pulls something from behind him, and when my eyes dart down, I'm confused.

"Thought I would surprise you with Reggie's smores bomb; he made a special batch for you."

I stare at the plate of dessert goodness, and for once, I'm slightly disappointed at the treat. "Oh… that's, uhm, sweet."

Wes sets the plate down as I stand in front of him. He grabs my hanging hands. "Thought we could have a night in, and as much as I wanted to set something up on the roof of Jupiter, well… Chicago winter just makes that a horrible idea." He smiles softly to himself.

"A night in is fine," I assure him blankly, unable to form facial expressions. "Shall I get us a bottle of wine from the kitchen?" I look off to the kitchen island.

The gentle circling of his thumbs on the back of my hands makes me refocus on him.

"Sure, but I'm hoping we can open the champagne." His grin spreads slightly. "You see, it's good that you moved in, but I'm not really liking this girlfriend title."

My pulse begins to quicken again. "Oh?" I choke out.

"No." He reaches into his pocket, and I almost can't stand

anymore, as I feel like I know what is about to happen. The fact a ring is being held up in front of me confirms that my instinct around this man is real.

"Emmy, we circled around one another for a few years, and I swear to you every night I looked at the sky and was reminded of you. Now, you're the only night I need, the only stars, and this sounds cheesy as fuck, but you are the one. You told me once when you were younger that I would get everything I ever wanted one day. You were right, but only if you are my wife. I want you to be my wife. Will you marry me?"

The hot flow of water down my cheeks as my smile doesn't fade only makes me cry more. "Yes! Yes, yes." I kneel down to kiss him, to let his arms wrap around me, for his fingers to put the ring on mine. "I love you."

"Me too, Emmy." We kiss for the next ten minutes until finally Wes convinces me that we need to open a bottle of champagne to celebrate.

He pours our glasses, and we clink. "You had no idea?"

"No clue. Why should I have known?"

That devilish grin of his comes out. "You didn't notice your notebook today?" His smug look remains on his face as he sips his drink.

I look at him, perplexed, yet have to grin. "You've been messing around in my notebook again?" I ditched post-its in favor of keeping everything in a small bullet journal. I'm too curious and quickly run to my purse to pull out my notebook. Returning, I turn pages like a maniac to find something out of the ordinary. I haven't looked at the book all day.

Turning, turning, ah… there it is. My to-do list for non-work-related things. His messy handwriting is apparent among my own.

Say yes

Looking up at Wes, I offer him a wide smile. "Were you ever concerned I would say no?"

He pulls me to him and plants us down on the sofa, causing a few drops of champagne to spill over the rim of my glass, but I don't mind, as I'm sitting on his lap. "No. But I love when you punish me for messing with your notebook."

I playfully pinch his arm before glancing at my champagne and taking a sip. "Sadie knew?"

"Of course, she helped me pick out the ring after I let her drag me through a baby store for two hours." He smiles, and I love that he secretly loved that. He and Sadie finally talked about their parents when she figured it out herself at Thanksgiving. To all our surprise, she wasn't bothered, nor saw her parents' marriage choice as a big deal.

"I guess we need to plan a wedding to avoid her due date. Funny enough, the Olive Owl sent me a newsletter about booking spots for a spring wedding… or is that too fast?"

He tops up my glass. "No. We could get on a plane to Vegas tomorrow and it still won't be fast enough. Plan away."

"Oh, man, I hope I don't get too sidetracked with our wedding on top of all the events for work."

Wes grins at me as he takes my other hand. "But, Emmy, you like distractions when I'm involved," he reminds me with flashing eyes.

I kiss his cheek and murmur approval, as everything he says is all completely true.

———

6 MONTHS LATER

A deep breath escapes me as my nerves go in all directions in my body. Staring into the long mirror, an overwhelming feeling comes over me that I will only ever have this once. The view of me in a long curve-hugging dress with a layer of meshed lace over top, a gold belt around my waist, and a plunging neckline that I debated with my mother for a good two hours over. My hair half up and my makeup natural. All exactly what I envisioned for my day—slightly boho and chic.

The bouquet of peach-colored roses is placed in my hands, and I look to my side to see a beaming Sadie smiling at me.

"So, I guess I can call you my sister."

I can't help but smile brightly. "Yeah."

Already my heart is full and happy that today is the day I become someone's wife. I can't wait to see Wes waiting at the end of the aisle… waiting for me.

"Let's head in there."

Sadie laughs as she straightens my long veil. "Someone is eager. We still have five minutes."

"Okay, what's a few minutes more," I comment and admire Sadie for being a perfect maid of honor, despite the fact that any week she is going to pop out a baby boy. I made sure to leave a basket of foot lotions, fuzzy socks, and massage oil in her room, as everyone is staying over at the Olive Owl farm tonight.

"I forgot to check with the staff about the fire—"

Sadie interrupts me. "Stop it. You are not a planner today, and yes, the fire is coming. Ruby mentioned she saw them building the fire-pit outside for later, and I am confident she and Cole fooled around behind the barn too."

I smile in relief, as we decided to add marshmallow roasting to after-dinner treats, in addition to our wedding cake of a tower of donuts.

"Oh, and I have this…" Sadie says as she grabs a small box from her bag. Returning to me, she hands me the box. "Something new."

I unwrap the white ribbon around the navy-blue box, lift the lid, and have to laugh at the lacy garter belt. "Wow, this is…" I'm not sure how to respond.

"Yeah, I know, slightly awkward that my brother will be taking that off you, but I do need to fulfill my maid-of-honor duties and, well… Logan said my brother should be happy." Her eyes go bold before she takes the garter and swings it around her finger. She moves to bend over but stops. "Sorry, I didn't think about how I'm going to get this on you. I'm an elephant in a dress." She tries a few more positions but realizes she is too far along to comfortably bend over and help my dress up.

"Don't worry, I can do this," I assure her and sling my leg up to rest my foot on the dresser. Sadie brings the garter to my foot, and she slides it up my leg before correcting my dress as I rest my foot back down.

"Now you're set," she promises, and I see she's getting emotional.

"Don't make me cry, I don't want Wes marrying a raccoon." Because really, mascara already running is not ideal.

Sadie exhales loudly. "Okay, no crying."

I nod and touch her shoulders.

"Let's go get me married."

———

WALKING down the aisle outside at the farm, I don't notice all thirty people staring at me. My eyes are glued to Wes who is standing at the end of what feels like the world's longest aisle. Holy smokes, he looks sexy as sin in a three-piece suit. He mouths *wow* to me, with his eyes having a glint meant only for me.

The rustic theme of our wedding fits the setting on this warm spring day.

Every step to Wes feels tiny, as if I can't get to him fast enough. I completely forget that my father is walking me down the aisle. I'm only reminded when I see Sadie in front of me hugging her brother then taking a spot up front.

"Who gives this woman to this man?"

"I do," my father says, and when I glance at him, I see tears. He hugs me before shaking Wes's hand.

And then it happens.

Wes with a roguish grin takes my hand to guide me to stand in front of him. The touch of our skin igniting flutters to roam around my heart.

"Here we are," I whisper, and I feel absolutely giddy.

"We are." In a flash he pulls me to him and his mouth plants on mine. He dips me back and this is all a surprise. To the guests too, and I hear the faint *awws* and laughs.

"Uhm, young man, normally you do that after the vows," the justice of the peace, a man in his fifties wearing glasses, reminds us.

Keeping me leaned back, Wes quickly side-glances to the man. "Nah, I can't wait for that. Not with this one." Wes gives me a wicked look before he kisses me again. A long, smooth, confirming kiss which I return to the fullest.

Bringing me back up, I already know my lips are swollen, and I try to steady my breathing. He interlaces our fingers as we re-focus our attention.

"Since the young man doesn't want to follow protocol, how do you wish to proceed?"

"Fast. Let's do this fast so we can call her my wife," Wes eagerly replies.

Everyone laughs, and I can't ease my glowing smile. "I agree. Let's do the quick version. I've already been dreaming about this for years."

Wes leans in and lets our foreheads touch before he whispers, "The best type of dream, but I'm not a dream."

"No, you're not. You're my husband," I lament.

"And you're my wife."

The justice of the peace clears his throat again. "Not quite husband and wife. Shall we get through this?"

We both quickly nod, and the next two minutes speed by. It's almost a blur. It's only when I hear whistling and clapping as Wes's lips land on my own that I have the confirmation.

"Let's get out of here," he mutters against the skin near my ear.

"Positive we have a wedding reception to attend," I reply in the same manner.

"Emmy, you made us go traditional for the past week. I *need* to be inside you. Take you as my wife."

I wink at him. "*Oh,* that's happening. I allotted in time for wearing something really distracting when we go to bed tonight."

It makes him chuckle softly before the tips of our noses nip one another as we both grin.

"Sounds perfect," he informs me before linking our hands and guiding us back down the aisle together, as husband and wife.

THANK YOU

Readers, I hope you enjoyed this second chance tale.

Lindsay, as always a delight on the editing front.

Brittni, thanks for reading in the early rough stages.

To Lindsey, for your cover magic.

ARC and bookstagram readers, you are little stars. Can't release a book without you. I am so thankful!

That music playlist and the repeat button, you helped me keep moving along!

My significant other and offspring, this one involved a lot of coffee during early mornings in an already strange year. Thanks for letting me make it happen. Writer of kissing books is probably not what you both had in mind when this all started…

www.ingramcontent.com/pod-product-compliance
Lightning Source LLC
Chambersburg PA
CBHW060400310726
48976CB00003B/896